Singles 101

Also by A'ndrea J. Wilson

Wife 101

Husband 101

Couples 101

Four Seasons of Love: A Romance Anthology

Ready & ABLE Teens: Ebony's Bad Habit

Ready & ABLE Teens: Desiree Dishes the Dirt

My Business His Way: Wisdom & Inspiration for Entrepreneurs

Kiss & Tell: Releasing Expectations

Singles 101

A'ndrea J. Wilson

The Wife 101 Series ✿ Book 4

Divine
Garden
Press

Published by Divine Garden Press, LLC
PO Box 371
Soperton, GA 30457

ISBN-13: 978-0615991764
ISBN-10: 0615991769
Library of Congress Control Number: 2014909966
Cover Design & Interior Layout: A'ndrea J. Wilson
Cover Photography: The Snappy Diva (www.thesnappydiva.com)

Scripture used is taken from either the King James Version or Amplified Version of the Bible unless otherwise indicated.

Scripture taken from THE AMPLIFIED BIBLE, Old Testament copyright © 1065, 1987 by the Zondervan Corporation. The Amplified New Testament copyright © 1958, 1987 by The Lockman Foundation. Used by permission.

Scripture taken from The Holy Bible, King James Version, Old and New Testament copyright © 1984, 1977 by Thomas Nelson, Inc.

For my unmarried readers who have waited patiently. Being single is not a curse; it's an adventure. Know that through God you can scale and move mountains.

For verily I say unto you, That whosoever shall say unto this mountain, Be thou removed, and be thou cast into the sea; and shall not doubt in his heart, but shall believe that those things which he saith shall come to pass; he shall have whatsoever he saith. (Mark 11:23)

March

Lesson 1: Can You Trust God When It All Falls Down?

For my thoughts are not your thoughts, neither are your
ways my ways, saith the Lord.
(Isaiah 55:8)

Tisha

I might not have had a loving husband or precious children, but what I did have was the perfect career. That was the benefit of being man-less and childless—I got to do what I wanted to do, when I wanted to do it. No questions, no compromises, just all me, all day, every day. And let's be honest; who really doesn't want the world to revolve around themselves?

It's not that I didn't eventually want marriage, and maybe a drooling kid or two wouldn't have been that bad; however, I realized that the moment I say "I do," life as I knew it—and loved it—would come to an end. I'd have to put others' needs before my own . . . Eww. I guess God would have to work on my heart in that area. He changed my best friend, Amber Ross-Hayes, and she was a straight mess, so I was sure he could manage a slightly narcissistic woman like me. But now that I've thought about it, Amber had always been a closet romantic. She'd bought into the fairytale, happily ever after notion that some sappy woman created ages ago. It made perfect sense that she was the first to marry out of the two of us. She'd even attended this Wife 101 class at her church to learn how to get and keep a man. Although I wasn't interested in any class called Wife 101, I felt a little left out when she hid her enrollment from me, but I got over it quickly. The class must have worked because she ended up dating and marrying her employee, Eric Hayes. At first, I thought she was insane for fraternizing with the help. Not only was he poor, he also had a child from a previous relationship. I tried to talk some sense into her, but the girl was in love, so she chose him over more qualified candidates, including a very wealthy mogul named Jonathan Gold who had given her an enviable engagement ring. Personally, I would have married Gold for the ring alone, but Amber's do-the-right-thing attitude mixed with her affection for Eric caused her to give Gold his ring back—ladies, never give the ring back. At the time, I was ready to call mental health services on Amber because I was convinced that she had lost her mind. Nevertheless, Amber's love for Eric has never wavered and I've come around to liking him—for the most part. He treats her well and they seem to have a good life together, so who was I to judge?

But I wanted more from my life. I wanted to be at the top of my career, and I wanted my man to be my equal. I didn't have time to clean a man up and train him to meet my needs like Amber did. She went through all kinds of stress fooling with Eric and the mother of his child. Had the girl up in court, fighting for joint custody, and airing all of their dirty laundry. Not me—I couldn't handle that much drama. Plus, she had to make him the CEO of one of her businesses just so he could feel like a man. Uh umm. Tisha didn't do charity cases. If a man wanted to even spend five minutes with me, I needed to see his résumé, credit score, and a copy of last year's taxes.

I'd dated quite a bit, but I still hadn't found the one—or he hadn't found me. So what does a woman in her thirties who is single do? You guessed it—I focused on my career. Over a span of fifteen years I'd gone from being a middle school teacher to a high school teacher to a vice principal to a principal, and now my eyes were set on the job of a regional superintendent. I was a shoe-in for the position—I had all of the qualifications. I was a certified teacher with ten years of classroom experience. I was rounding off my fifth year as principal and my school, Turner Hill High, had the highest standardized test scores amongst high schools in the county. I'd earned Bachelors' degrees in Education and English, a Master's degree in Educational Leadership, and an Education Specialist degree in Educational Leadership and Administration. In addition, I'd won Teacher of the Year at the school and county level during my fourth year of teaching. If I was promoted to a regional superintendent position, I promised myself I would immediately begin work towards a Ph.D. It was unnecessary to have both an Ed.S. and a Ph.D., but I wanted the degree anyway. I loved my job, but more importantly, I loved being the best.

At that moment, my very best self was seated inside the office of Dr. Joel Cooper, the current superintendent of schools in DeKalb County and of course, my boss. We had been in conversation about the possibility of me transitioning into a senior administrator role. I'd expressed my interest months ago, and was anticipating getting the nod of approval from both Dr. Cooper and the school board. My curriculum vitae was impeccable and there were very few principals in the Metro Atlanta area that could outshine me.

I'd been expecting further communication from Dr. Cooper about the job, so I didn't blink when I received a call from him earlier in the week, requesting a face-to-face meeting with me. I assumed our conference would be a confirmation of his intentions to recommend me for the position of regional superintendent at an upcoming school board meeting. Dressed for the part, I strolled sophisticatedly into his office wearing a brand new black and white power suit and black designer pumps. Like a true pro, I greeted him with a firm handshake and took a seat across from him at his invitation to sit.

Which brings me to that moment—my "very best self" moment. The moment that will always and forever be seared into my memory as the time Dr. Cooper tried to play me like an amateur.

"I realize that you desire to move from your current placement as principal at Turner Hill High to the opening as a regional superintendent," he said as he leaned back in his chair and determinedly scratched his five o'clock shadow, the pesky hairs budding mercilessly on his lower jawline. I eyed the defiant facial stubble that seemed both to irritate him and distract his attention from our extremely important conversation.

When he didn't immediately continue his statement, I prodded him on. "Yes, I do. We've discussed this on several occasions."

"Yes, yes, we have," he said, removing his fingers from his face and refocusing on the matter at hand. "You've done well at Turner Hill, but I'm not quite sure that placing you in senior administration is the right move for you at this time."

Although I'm a professional, I've never been good at pretending or holding my tongue. "I beg your pardon?" I asked. It was all I could do not to flip his desk over on him. Up until this point, he had given me every indication that I was the perfect candidate for the promotion. Now, all of a sudden I was unworthy? It didn't make sense.

He straightened up in his chair and folded his hands on the desk in front of him. "Please don't misunderstand. It's not that you are underperforming, it's just that your unique skills may be better served elsewhere in the district."

I was offended. I could see where this conversation was leading and I didn't like it one bit. "I'm certain my performance levels are not being questioned," I said firmly. "Under my leadership, my school has had the highest Georgia High School Writing Test and Georgia High School Graduation Test scores in the county, not to mention, one of the highest in the state. And as I recall, when I taught eighth Grade English, my school had the highest Criterion-Referenced Competency Test scores in the county. So please explain to me why the word underperforming is even on the table, why my promotion to regional superintendent isn't a good idea, and where else my skills would be better served."

"Miss Dawson, my mention of underperformance was to say that this is not the case with you. I didn't mean to imply that the quality of your work was an issue," he said, trying to calm me down.

But there would be no appeasing of me, not when the rug was being pulled out from under my feet. "Then what exactly is the issue?"

He cleared his throat. I could tell he was nervous which meant the next thing he was going to say was likely to send me over the edge. "I believe that we have a school that is in dire need of someone like you—someone with the kind of leadership skills you possess."

There it was. No one in their right mind made a lateral career move. "Are you saying that you want me to be a principal somewhere else? Which school?"

He nodded. "Yes, that's what I'm saying. I think you'd be very effective at Ponce De Leon Alternative High School."

I let out a facetious laugh. "This is a joke, right? Am I on hidden camera or something?" I looked around the room, hoping a camera crew would dash in from out of nowhere and inform me that this was all a prank.

His face tightened. "Not at all. I'm very serious."

My smile vanished and reality set in. He wanted to send me to the worst high school in the city. He wanted me to fail. "Wow. So after fifteen years of hard work and dedication I get demoted to working at an alternative school. This can't be real."

"Miss Dawson, this is not a demotion," he said persuasively. "You'll still be a principal and you'll be charged with using your skills to create positive change in a poorly performing school. I thought you would view this as a challenge. If you can turn Ponce De Leon Alternative around, it would demonstrate to me and the school board that you are ready for senior administration."

I rolled my eyes, unable and unwilling to be nice about the demise of my career in education. "A challenge? More like a death sentence. Let me ask you something, Dr. Cooper. Of your four current regional superintendents, how many of them were asked to prove themselves by taking on a failing school?"

"Well none, but—"

I interrupted him. "That's what I thought."

He frowned. "Miss Dawson, I don't think you're being a team player. Willingness to take on difficult projects for the sake of the system is one of the qualities I'm looking for in a regional superintendent."

I stood up. I was mentally and emotionally exhausted from this conversation. I needed to exit the room quickly before the ounce of diplomacy that I had left abandoned me, and he came face to face with the girl that used to beat up on boys just because I could. "With all due respect, please don't Miss Dawson me again. I know the game, Dr. Cooper. Don't treat me like a novice because I've been in this system for way too long. Either you or someone else doesn't want me to climb any higher than I already am, so you're sending me on an impossible mission. Believe me when I say that I won't go quietly. You better find someone else to clean-up Ponce De Leon, because Miss Dawson is not interested."

I rang Amber's doorbell three times in a row. When no one answered, I rang it three times more. I knew she and the hubby were home because their cars were in the driveway.

Eric yanked open the door, obviously irritated by my relentless ringing. "Would you lay off the doorbell?" he asked. "We've got a sleeping baby in here, and if you wake him up, you're taking him to your house with you and you can deal with all of the nonstop crying."

"Hello to you too, Eric. I see who isn't getting any sleep at night."

"You have no idea. Take my advice and don't have any children."

"I'll definitely take that under consideration. Where's your wife?"

"In her office, trying to get some work done while junior is passed out."

"The joys of parenthood."

"Don't remind me." He stepped out of the doorway and allowed me entry. "Go on back."

I headed to the rear of the house where Amber had converted a downstairs bedroom into a stylish home office. Now that Amber was a full-time mommy, she had very little free time to visit the two companies she still ran, so she worked primarily from home.

"Knock, knock," I said as I entered her office through the already opened door.

"Hey," she said, barely glancing up from her computer screen to greet me.

I hated to say it, but the woman looked horrendous. Half of her hair was pulled back into a ponytail, and the other half was sticking straight up into the air in every direction. She had milk and food stains on her gray jersey knit sweater, and the crusty stuff around her eyes was a clear indication that she had not showered yet today despite the fact that it was going on 5:00 p.m.

I sat down in a comfortable wingback chair she had in the corner and propped my feet up on the ottoman. She'd added this chair in the office once Eric Jr. had been born so that she could feed him without leaving the room. Outside of her desk and chairs, the home office also contained a couple of file cabinets, bookshelves, a TV, and a playpen.

"What's up?" Amber asked, finally turning away from the laptop.

"I hate him."

"Who? Clyde?"

I rolled my eyes. Clyde was a guy I'd been seeing off and on for several months. He was nothing serious, just company when I felt bored or lonely. "No! As if I care enough about Clyde to hate him. I'm talking about Joel."

"Joel?"

"Dr. Cooper, my boss."

"Oh. The superintendent. Why? What did he do to you? Is this about that promotion?"

"Yes. He's trying to downgrade me to being a principal at Ponce De Leon Alternative. Do I look like I belong at an alternative school to you?"

Her face morphed from an expression of concern into a grimace. "Oh no! Are you serious? That school is a mess."

I folded my arms in front of me like a kid who couldn't get the toy she wanted. "Exactly what I told him. He must have me confused for a sucker. There's no way I'm going to work there. I'll quit and start my own charter school before I set foot inside of Ponce De Leon."

Amber smiled. "That's actually not a bad idea. You could do it."

I rolled my eyes again. "I forgot I was talking to Mrs. I-own-my-own-businesses-and-everyone-else-should-too. Honestly, I don't feel like going through the whole trouble of starting my own school. Unlike you, I like working for someone else. I just want to advance in my career. I progress forward. I don't do standing still, and I definitely don't do moving backwards."

Shrugging, Amber said, "So what are you going to do? Is he willing to reconsider?"

I sighed. The entire situation was a nightmare and I just wanted to wake up. "I don't know. I told him I wasn't going to

Ponce and left before he could saying anything else dumb to me. I was so ready to flip out and tear that place up."

"I bet you were. I'm proud of you for leaving because I would have hated to bail you out of DeKalb County Jail."

I smirked. "Me too. Orange jumpsuits don't work well with my shape and skin tone."

Amber laughed.

"Amber, I am so disappointed," I whined. "I just knew that job was mine. And it's not like these positions open up all of the time. Someone has to quit, get fired, or die before I'll have another chance to move up."

She nodded as if she understood. "Why don't you apply at another school district? Atlanta's a big metropolis with plenty of opportunities."

I let out a moan. "I know, but I've spent fifteen years working in this district. I know everything about this system and I'm comfortable. I'd hate to have to start all over again."

"I get it, but sometimes you just have to move out of your comfort zone in order to have something better. Look, have you thought about going to the singles conference with my church?"

I should have known she would somehow slip an invite to her church into the conversation. She'd been trying to get me to attend a service at her church for years now with no luck. Not that I wasn't a Christian, I just wasn't religious. I believed in God, prayed, and read my Bible from time to time, but hanging out at church every Sunday wasn't my thing. Amber wasn't a religious zealot by any means, but she really was into her particular church and the various activities they hosted. This summer, they were supposedly hosting a singles conference which Amber and Eric had helped coordinate.

"Not really," I said. "I know you're all into attending those Christian classes, but I'm not sure they're right for me."

"How do you know if you won't try? Plus, the conference is going to be in Las Vegas. Tell me that doesn't sound exciting to you. I'll be there teaching a workshop so you won't be alone.

It will be fun. And it will help take your mind off this whole job thing."

Maybe she had a point. I did need a vacation and to get away from this whole alternative school problem. Vegas would be fun, especially if I had my best friend with me—unless her husband consumed all of her time. "Is Eric going?"

Amber nodded. "As if I would leave my husband here with all of these shameless Atlanta women. He and I both need a break from these children. Plus, he's also teaching a workshop—a single father's class or something like that. Come on, Tisha! The cutoff date for early registration is in a couple of weeks. I promise you will have a good time."

I felt myself caving in. "When is this conference anyway?"

"June 1st. It's perfect timing because you'll be done with the school year. Think about it—five days in Las Vegas, Nevada, the second city that never sleeps. And since it's a singles conference, I'm sure there will be plenty of good looking men there from all over the country. The Woods are doing it grand this time. It won't just be my church, but singles from everywhere."

An image of me in front of a slot machine with a crew of handsome men surrounding me flashed through my mind. "Good looking, single men?"

"Could be," she said, smiling.

I hated Amber. She always knew the right thing to say to persuade me to go along with her silly plans. If this Vegas thing didn't work out, I was going to defriend her. I sighed and conceded. "Okay, I'm in."

Lesson 2: Few Things Are Forever

Heaven and earth shall pass away: but my words shall not pass away. Luke 21:33

Nelson

Why did bad things always happen to me when I was minding my own business? I'll admit, I'm not the perfect guy and I have done my fair share of dirt, but it seemed like every time I was on the right path, some unexpected snag tripped me up and sent me looking for retribution.

I'd gotten off work and headed to the gym to lift weights with a few friends of mine. I was about ten miles away from my destination when my cell phone rang; an unknown number popped up on the screen. Thinking it was the guys trying to let me know they would be late, I accepted the call, saying, "Whaddup?"

"Hel-Hello?" a shaky, feminine voice answered. The voice sounded a little familiar, but I couldn't make an exact match. I had dated so many women over the years, that unless it was someone recent, I wouldn't have been able to guess anyway.

"Who's this?" I asked, getting straight to the point. Rule number one in the player's handbook: Always maintain control over the situation.

"Still a straight shooter. I see some things haven't changed in all of these years," she said, not answering my question.

"Who is this?" I asked again, this time with a hint of aggression in my voice.

The caller sighed. "It's Charmaine."

My heartbeat quickened. It couldn't be. "Charmaine? Charmaine who?" I asked, trying to sound cool and composed, but the truth was, I was completely shaken up.

"Don't act like you don't know me. It's Charmaine West."

Hearing that name made my blood boil. Charmaine was the reason I didn't trust women; the reason I never married, never had kids. After she cheated on me with a football player named Brandon back in college, then got pregnant by him and married the guy, I'd sworn off love and commitment for the rest of my life. My lips curled in indignation. "How did you get my number?" I asked coldly.

She let out a light giggle. "I have my ways."

I shook my head and huffed. There was only one person in the world that would give her my cell phone number. "Let me guess. Gerald," I said, referring to my old college roommate.

"Good guess."

I made a mental note to slap Gerald upside the head the next time I saw him. The man-code specifically stated that one never, ever gave out pertinent information to a woman, especially an ex without permission. I would certainly deal with Gerald later, but at that moment, Charmaine was on my line and I had no clue why she was going out of her way to reach me after over two decades of silence. "What do you want?"

"O-kay. I'm sensing a lot of hostility coming from you. Are you still mad at me after all of this time? It's been what? Twenty-five years or so since we broke up." Her voice came across confident, yet labored as if she had a bad cold or the flu.

Sure, it was a long time to hold a grudge, but heartbreak isn't something men like me got over quickly. I shrugged as if she could see me over the phone and said, "Something like that. I'm not mad, I'm just not interested in small talk. So, what do you want?"

She sighed again. "There's no easy way to say this, so I'll just come out with it . . ."

I held my breath and waited for her announcement, hopping it wouldn't be something that would push the dagger further into my back. After "I cheated," "I'm pregnant," and "I'm marrying him," what more could this woman need to tell me?

"I have cancer."

That wasn't what I expected. I thought she was going to tell me some wild, *Maury* TV show mess like the paternity test results were in and her 24-year-old son was really my child. But she had cancer? As much as I wanted to hate her, I couldn't help but feel devastated. "I'm sorry to hear that. I sincerely hope you beat the disease."

"I won't. It has spread from my throat to other areas of my body. There's not much the doctors can do at this point. It's terminal." She sniffled. A moment ago she sounded strong, but now I could hear the tears in her voice.

A wave of emotions overtook me and panic gripped the parts of my mind that had previously loathed Charmaine. "So what are you saying? You're gonna die?" I didn't mean for my words to come out so quickly and loud, but her grave confession had completely blown my cool composure.

Charmaine cleared her throat. "Well, we all die eventually. I'm just going to die sooner than I thought."

"How soon?"

"Soon. They've given me thirty days."

I punched the steering wheel in front of me. Thirty days? This couldn't be true. "How can they say something like that? I hate doctors. How do they know how long anyone is going to live?"

"Nelson," she said with more strength in her voice, "this time, they're right. My health is failing me pretty quickly. I look and feel horrible. The cancer is aggressive and . . . I didn't call you to make you feel sorry for me. Death has a way of forcing you to make amends with those you've wronged. I–I just wanted to apologize to you for the way I treated you back in college. I really did love you—I still do—but you and I just weren't meant to be. I should have handled it better. I should have been more careful with your heart, and I am deeply sorry for any pain that I caused you."

"You don't have to—"

"Yes, I do. I want to meet my Maker in peace, knowing that I took responsibility for my mistakes and at least tried to seek forgiveness."

A few warm tears trickled down my face. "Where's—How's Brandon?" Although I despised the man, I never wished something this horrible on him.

"He's managing. This is very difficult for him to accept, but he is trying to be strong for my sake, and for the sake of our kids."

"Does he know you're calling me?"

"Yeah. He understands why this is important to me. I'm not sure when I'll . . . Please promise me that you'll come to the funeral—if you can. My sisters will notify you of the arrangements. It would really mean a lot to me to know that you cared enough to come." I could tell that she was crying, and the thought of it all caused more tears to escape my own eyes.

"I—Of course, I'll come. I can't believe this is happening to you. As much as I was upset about us, I never wanted . . ."

"I know." She sniffled again. "You're a good man, Nelson. I just hope that you didn't let what I did to you ruin the way you look at relationships. Gerald told me that you never married and were sort of a player. That's not the Nelson I knew. It makes me think that I had something to do with how much you've changed. If I did, please forgive me, and please open your heart to love again."

I sat in my car feeling overwhelmed by all that she had said. I had waited 25 years for her to truly apologize, and now that she was, it didn't feel nearly as freeing as I'd imagined it would. Instead, I felt as if I had wasted the last 25 years of my life being bitter instead of living. I wished I could turn back time and do it all over again, but now, it was too late. The only woman I have ever been in love with was about to die.

"Listen, I have to go," she said, pulling me away from my regret. "Some of my family just came over to see me. It was so good to hear your voice again. Thank you for listening and not hanging up on me. I pray that God gives you everything your heart desires. I love you, Nelson."

"I–I love you too, Charmaine," I said weakly.

"Goodbye, Nelson."

"Goodbye, Charmaine."

I couldn't remember the last time I broke down, but at the sound of the phone disconnecting, I couldn't stop the scream that arose from my mouth.

A little over two weeks later, I stood in front of Charmaine's white casket with my brother, Eric, at my side. Her face was the same as I remembered, just a bit older and much thinner. But she was still beautiful and way too young to be dead. It was hard to fathom that less than three weeks ago I had heard her voice so clearly, and she was alive. Now, she was gone, and what remained of her body was lying in a casket in front of me inside of a medium-sized church in Greenwood, South Carolina.

I felt Eric's hand grip my shoulder and squeeze gently, attempting to comfort me. I choked back a few tears—it wasn't my style to cry, especially in front of other people. Wiping my eyes, I looked over at my brother who nodded at me, letting me know that it was okay to feel the pain. The line of loved ones who wanted to view the body was increasing, so I said my final goodbye with a single kiss on her forehead, took three seconds to view her face one last time, and turned to walk away. Brandon was sitting on the front pew, his hands covering his face. I noticed their three children, two adult males, and one teenaged girl, sitting beside him—all wearing forlorn expressions. As I walked past Brandon, I patted him on his back. He looked up at me with swollen eyes, standing instantly upon recognizing my face.

"Your family is in our prayers," Eric said, after we had stood there for a few moments and I had not found the words to say.

Brandon nodded at Eric. Speechless, I stepped toward him and gave him a man-hug which consisted of a half hug, half pat on the back, and a handshake. Brandon participated in the symbol of brotherhood, then nodded at me before Eric and I continued to walk down the aisle, further and further away from Charmaine.

In the car, during the three hour drive back to Atlanta, Eric tried his best to cheer me up through old school music and forcing me to reminisce about our childhood. I was surprised that he was willing to talk about the times that I had beat him up or tricked him out of his money, since prior to this, he always acted as if he resented me for it. After several bittersweet "remember when" stories, he said, "I'm really sorry about Charmaine. I know she meant a lot to you."

"Yeah, she did," I said. "Thanks for coming with me. I'm not sure if I would have had the courage to do it alone."

Eric nodded. "Anytime, man. Listen, I have an idea. Why don't you come with us to Vegas this summer?"

My curiosity was instantly peaked. What grown man didn't want to go to Vegas? "Vegas? As in Las Vegas, Nevada?"

"The one and only."

"You and Amber don't gamble. What are you guys going to Vegas for?"

"Our church is having a singles conference there."

I groaned. "Okay, now it make sense. I should have known it was something with that church. But if it's a singles conference, why are you and Amber going? Y'all ain't single."

"We helped organize it, we're one of the sponsors, and we're each teaching a workshop during the conference—that's why we're going."

"I see," I said, considering the invitation. I hadn't been to Vegas in years. Last time I'd gone, the boys and I had a blast. Another wild trip to Vegas could certainly help me get over Charmaine's death, but I wasn't sure about going with Eric and Amber . . . and their church? "Wait, hold up! You're telling me that a church is having a singles conference in Las Vegas? They want to take a bunch of single Christians to Sin City? Are they stupid?"

Eric chuckled. "No, they're not stupid. I know it's a bit unorthodox, but they rarely do anything in the typical fashion. Remember a year and a half ago when Amber and I went to the marriage retreat in South Beach, Miami? It was a crazy idea, but it worked—well. They had this whole theory of throwing us into the lion's den. They figured if our marriages could survive in hedonism, they could survive in the real world. They more than likely have the same idea about doing a singles event in Vegas."

I let out a much needed laugh.

"Bro, I must admit, I'm not one for going to churches outside of our family's church, but that church you and Amber attend seems like it's cool as h—"

Eric scowled, his expression stopping me mid-sentence.

"How are you going to say that word and church in the same sentence? Nelson, you are so disrespectful. And another thing, the place Hell is not cool, it's flaming hot. Keep it up and you just might end up there."

I snickered. "Whoa! Sorry, Pastor Hayes. I didn't mean to offend you. I'm just saying that your church seems cool."

"Very funny. You know I'm not a preacher, I'm just telling you to watch your mouth. So, do you want to go to Vegas or not?"

I shrugged, still feeling on the fence about the matter. "Meh, I don't know. I'd love to go to L.V., but hanging with y'all Christians might suck all the fun out of it."

Eric smiled. "Hardly. Do you know how many attractive, single women are going to be there? Think about it."

My eyebrows rose. "Vegas, summertime, *and* single women? Where do I sign up?"

Lesson 3: Get Over It

Will he reserve *his anger* for ever? Will he keep *it* to the end? Behold, thou hast spoken and done evil things as thou couldest. (Jeremiah 3:5)

Lena

Who should be labeled as a chronic failure in relationships? Me. At 37-years-old, I was headed toward the life of a spinster. I definitely wanted my happily ever after—to get married and stay married—but every time I opened my heart to love and companionship, the bottom fell out and I ended up with more crushed dreams and heavier emotional baggage. I had been in a slew of long-term relationships—including one with my child's father, Eric Hayes—and had even been married once, yet I was still left despising the fact that I was stuck with my maiden name. Being Miss Henry felt permanent like an ugly birthmark that was too large to cover up.

My first mistake was getting married too young. Fresh out of high school, I ignored the advice of my family and married my high school sweetheart, Tony Hart. Huge lapse in judgment. Tony was a decent guy and at the time, I thought I loved him, but neither of us had a clue of what it took to have a successful marriage or adult life. Two years into the marriage we were sinking fast. I could tell by the look in Tony's eyes that he wanted to be free, to be young, and find himself. Truth be told, I was still searching for my identity as well. After a dramatic separation following a bunch of arguing, lies, and late nights, we officially ended the marriage. I had not even celebrated my 21st birthday. My brief stint as Mrs. Hart ended before I had a chance to see the name plastered across the left-hand side of a personal check.

Then along came Eric. He was special. I knew from our first interaction that I could easily fall in love with him. He wasn't like many of the men I met—irresponsible, prideful, or lustful. He had been raised well; a good Christian home, two caring parents, rules and boundaries—you know, the makings of a well-rounded individual. I wanted so badly to be a part of something bigger than myself that I practically dove into a relationship with him. We moved too fast, engaging in premarital sex without considering the ramifications. When I found out that I was pregnant with Jonelle, I just knew that Eric would marry me. I was wrong. He wasn't ready for marriage and even worse, he was overly obligated to his family. It was difficult for him to fully give himself to a relationship with me and Jonelle because he couldn't detach himself from his parents. After trying every trick in the book I knew to get him to change, I became frustrated and walked away from the relationship. Who knew that ten years later he would turn into Super-dad and Super-husband for another woman—Amber Ross-Hayes.

I'll admit, I was jealous. It didn't seem fair. Why did Eric get to have the happy family? Why did he get primary custody of Jonelle? Why did he marry her when he could have married me? Why did I seem to always get the short end of the stick?

Okay, so I wasn't very nice during our custody battle, and yes, I orchestrated a big scene with a fake fiancé and some client of his that was obsessed with him, but it was all in an attempt to keep my baby, Jonelle, with me. She was my world, all that I truly had that meant something to me. I just didn't want to lose her, especially to the man who had let me down so greatly. But somehow, in the end, I lost her anyway.

Almost three and a half years later, things had changed in some ways, but were still the same in others. Eric and I had gone back to court and now had a better joint custody agreement. Both parties had agreed to Jonelle living half of the year with Eric and the other half with me. Because we lived in the same county, she was able to continue attending the same school which helped keep her life consistent. From January 1st to June 30th, she stayed with Eric during the week and I had her on the weekends. From July 1st to December 31st, she lived with me and Eric got her on the weekends. We alternated holidays. So far, the new custody agreement was working well. Anything was better than me being the noncustodial parent.

As far as Eric and I were concerned, our relationship had grown from cold to cordial. Eric tried to be kind to me, but for some reason, I couldn't completely shake the bitterness I had toward him. I felt so cheated by the way my life had turned out, him being one of my major disappointments. I'd dated quite a bit since him, but each guy seemed worse than the last. There was *always* something wrong with the men I dated—too many kids, too many excuses, too many women on the side, too many teeth in their mouths, too insecure, too clingy, too broke, too ugly, too ignorant, and just too much. Every man I met was too something, including the guy I was currently getting to know who was too annoying. His name was Douglass Powers. I'd been seeing him off and on for the past six months. He was a fairly attractive guy and he had a decent job, but I just wasn't seriously interested in him. To me, he was a bit corny, meaning he told silly jokes that only he thought were funny. He wasn't the most fashionable man, wearing old and outdated clothing that made him look as if he shopped at second hand stores. He treated me well, but sometimes I felt as if he expected too much from me. I didn't consider him my boyfriend, but he constantly tried to crowd me as if he owned me. I wanted to be married, but I wasn't desperate. As far as I was concerned, I would stay single rather than marry just anyone for the sake of being married. The whole dating process was frustrating. Often, I found myself thinking that perhaps if I had been more patient with Eric, we would be married instead of him and Amber.

Amber. I couldn't stand the woman. She thought she was the queen of England with her fancy house, expensive car, and booming businesses. Her perfection nauseated me. I was actually tickled pink when she was struggling to have a baby. At last, there was something she wasn't good at, something I had that she didn't. Unfortunately, her infertility issues didn't last too long. Now that she and Eric had their son, Eric Jr., I hoped they would back off my baby, Jonelle. To date, that hadn't happened.

It was a sunny Sunday afternoon in April and I had just parked my car in Eric's driveway to drop Jonelle back off at their house after my weekend visit. I hated parting ways with my little girl—actually she was quickly becoming a big girl. She was now 13, going on 14-years-old in August. I was already planning a big birthday party for her at Six Flags Over Georgia *without* the help of her father or stepmother. It would be a financial stretch to make it happen all by myself, but I was determined to show Mr. and Mrs. Moneybags that I too could give my daughter the best things in life. Since I wouldn't have weekday custody of Jonelle until July 1st, I had been taking extra shifts at the hospital where I worked as a nurse to save up the extra cash.

"Do you have everything, Jonnie?" I asked my daughter as she unbuckled her seatbelt and began gathering her overnight bag.

"Yes, ma'am," she replied back.

I touched the side of her innocent face, then leaned over and kissed her on the forehead. "Okay, let's get you inside."

We both exited my car and made our way to the Hayeses front door. Jonelle had a key to the house, but I always made her ring the doorbell when I returned her to Eric on Sunday evenings.

Eric answered the door within thirty seconds and Jonelle proceeded to give me a hug, give her father a hug, wave goodbye to me, and stroll inside the house—in that order.

We watched Jonelle's behavior, then Eric chuckled and said, "Thanks for dropping her off. I hope you two had a good weekend."

"We did. We always do," I responded curtly.

"Listen, I need to ask you a question. Do you mind stepping inside for a moment?" he asked politely.

I shrugged and walked into the house. My mind immediately began to race, considering all of the things he could possibly have to say to me. Were they moving out-of-state and wanted to take Jonelle with them? *Over my dead body!* Did they want to change our custody agreement? *Probably not.* Did he miss me? *Okay, I was getting carried away.*

I glanced around the foyer and peered into the living room of the house. Amber was nowhere to be seen which was a good thing. I personally felt that any conversation about Jonelle should remain between Eric and I—her actual birth parents.

"So, what's up? What did you want to ask?" I asked, getting straight to the point.

Eric exhaled and rubbed the back of his neck before saying, "Well, Amber and I are going on a trip in June for about a week. Since it's my half of the year, I can have Jonelle stay with my parents during that week and they can bring her to you on the weekends. Or, if you want, I am willing to let her stay with you during that week. I mean, her grandparents would love to spend the week with her, but I wanted to first give you the option of keeping her."

I folded my arms across my chest. "I see. Where you all going?"

"Las Vegas."

I blinked hard. This was not the answer I expected from him. "Vegas? You and Amber. I didn't think you all gambled."

"We don't. We're going to a singles conference with our church."

"But you're not single . . . unless I missed something and you two got a divorce."

Eric laughed. "No, we're a part of the event committee and we're also teaching a couple workshops during the conference. I'm praying it turns out well. I can't believe I actually got Nelson to sign up to go, but he thinks he's going to spend the entire time partying like a rock star."

The story was getting more and more surprising with each new detail. "Nelson's going too?"

"Yeah. Unimaginable, huh? Amber actually got her friend Tisha to register as well. I know God is moving if those two agreed to go to a church activity. I think the Woods actually hit the nail on the head when they decided to take this singles conference to Vegas. There'll probably be a lot of unlikely people there who really need a conference like this one."

I shook my head in disbelief. "You mean Amber's Tisha? The loud mouth one? She's going?"

"Yep. I am just as shocked as you are."

I couldn't help but feel slightly offended that I had been left out. "So why wasn't I invited? Oh, because I am supposed to stay here in Atlanta and babysit for you and your wife?"

Eric's eyes widen. It was a look he often gave me when he didn't know what to say. "I didn't think you would be interested," he muttered.

There was no way that Eric, Amber, and everyone else in Atlanta was going to Vegas and leaving me behind like a child. Nope, I wasn't having it. "Well, if everyone else is going to Vegas this summer, I'm going too. Why should you all get to have all of the fun? Don't I deserve some fun, too?"

Eric stepped back from me and put up his hands in a "stop" gesture. "Wait. Let me get this straight. You want to go with me and Amber to a singles conference in Las Vegas this summer?"

I placed my right hand on my hip. "Did I stutter?"

Eric shook his head and sighed. "Alright. If you wait here I'll go get the brochure so that you can register. Space is filling up fast, so you're going to have to call them right away."

Eric left me alone in the foyer and disappeared down the hallway. When he returned a few minutes later, he passed me a colorful brochure that provided general information about the conference. I flipped through it quickly, stopping at the figures for the conference and hotel fees. When I told Eric I wanted to go, I had not considered how expensive it might be to attend an event in Vegas. Although the price wasn't sky high, it was money that I had not budgeted for. In addition, the fees on the form did not include travel or miscellaneous expenses. In order to go, I would have to dip into Jonelle's birthday bash savings. I hated to "rob Peter to pay Paul," but Eric was staring at me and there was no way that I was going to back out now. I had to save face.

"Fine," I said. "Get your parents to watch the kids because I'm registering today. See you in Vegas," I said as I tapped the brochure against his chest and headed back out the front door.

June

Lesson 4: Life Rarely Happens As Expected

When I looked for good, then evil came *unto me*: and when I waited for light, there came darkness. (Job 30:26)

Tisha

My first mistake of the trip was letting Amber and Eric book my flight from Atlanta to Las Vegas. It was a four and a half hour, nonstop flight from Hartfield Jackson International Airport to McCarran International Airport via Airtran Airways—a ticket that set me back $450. Since I'm a bit impatient, I dislike flights that are more than an hour or two. I simply begin to get restless like little children in the backseat of a car during a family road trip. I thought I'd prepared myself well for the lengthy flight—bringing a few magazines I've been wanting to read, my iPod, and if all else failed, a book of Sudoku puzzles. But nothing I had gathered could have prepared me for being trapped in a window seat next to Nelson Hayes.

Amber had conveniently left out the part of our trip that included Nelson. As far as I knew, it would be just the cute couple (Amber and Eric) and me. I had gotten a mouthful from Amber about Eric's ex-girlfriend Lena also attending the conference, but from what I was told, she wasn't flying with us or expected to hang out with our group once we got there. Supposedly, she would just be another single person at the event. In my mind, I seriously doubted we would be free from run-ins with the chick, but I keep my negative thoughts to myself in an effort to save my best friend from further agitation. Amber couldn't stand the woman, and I understood why. Lena had a horrible attitude and had been a pain in Amber's butt since she and Eric had jumped the broom five years ago. Because my bestie didn't like her, I also pretended not to care for the woman, but secretly, I didn't care at all. Lena had never done anything to me personally, so why would I hate her? Woman-to-woman, I appreciated the fact that she loved her daughter and wasn't too keen on another lady trying to raise her child. Although I did feel that she should chill out with the whole angry woman vibe she had going, and I wasn't too pleased about the courtroom lie she had constructed during the custody case a few years back, Lena still had my sympathy. If I had a child by a man who wouldn't marry me and then years later he married someone else, I would be a tad hostile myself.

As I was saying, I was cognizant of Lena's appearance in Vegas, but I was completely taken aback by Nelson's. I had been in the presence of Nelson Hayes several times—Amber and Eric's wedding, the birth of E.J., and a few other special occasions where the Hayes clan had been invited. Eric and Nelson had the typical love-hate, sibling rivalry kind of relationship which prevented Eric from bringing him along when he and Amber went on social outings. From my limited interaction with Nelson, I was certain of one thing—I abhorred the man. There was something about him that got under my skin and frustrated me beyond belief. I wasn't used to someone rattling me so much, but he seemed to know exactly how to get on my last nerve without knowing me at all. With this in mind, sitting next to him on an airplane for four and a half hours was pure torture. Obviously the feeling was not mutual because he spent the entire time bothering me.

He arrived at the airport later than the rest of us, almost missing the flight. We had already boarded and taken our seats by the time he walked onto the plane, strolling down the aisle like he was GQ's Man of the Year. When he stopped at my row and flashed me a toothy grin, I wanted to die. No! I wanted to scream, but with such strict FAA regulations, I probably would have ended up being the one removed from the plane and banned from flying ever again.

He shoved his carry-on luggage into the overhead bin, shimmied past the elderly man in the aisle seat, and settled into the middle seat, clicking his seatbelt into place before speaking to me. "Tisha, so good to see you again. You're looking stunning, as always."

"Nelson," I replied tersely.

He sighed and smiled simultaneously as he was pleased with himself. "What are the odds that we'd be sitting together on this flight?"

I looked at him as if he were a fool. The question was certainly foolish. "Uh, about 100 percent if you also let Amber and Eric book your flight."

He nodded and pulled out his cell phone, tapping keys to shut it down. "Good point. Do you think they're trying to play matchmakers?"

The safety briefing had begun, but my mind was stuck on the idea of the Hayeses trying to hook Nelson and me up. Amber knew me well and I doubted she would stoop as low as to create a love connection between me and her disillusioned brother-in-law. Eric, on the hand, might want us to date, thinking it would either make Nelson grow up or at least get him out of his own hair. "I hope not. I didn't even know you were going to Vegas."

He peered at me smugly. "Really? I knew you were going. All I ask is that you not get jealous when you see these single women hanging all over me. I'm a little hard to resist."

I wanted to gag. "Trust me, jealously won't even be close to the emotion I'll be feeling. Happiness, relief, peace, and joy are more like it."

He rubbed his chin. "Don't act like you don't want me."

"I don't."

"Please, woman," he said then laughed. "I know your type."

This guy was a clown. I knew I was going to regret asking, but curiosity won over sensibility. "What exactly is my type?"

He licked his lips; I felt nauseated. "High maintenance, upwardly mobile professional, so-called independent woman who enjoys making a man beg for a few minutes of your time. You like being in control, but deep in your heart, you really want a man who you can't control."

I shifted in my seat. He'd pegged me correctly, but I wasn't going to give him the satisfaction of knowing it. "And I know your type, Nelson. You're an egotistical, immature, hormone-crazed male who thinks he's God's gift to women, but really is far from it. Stop trying to figure me out because no matter what you say or do, I will never be attracted to someone like you."

I thought he would be embarrassed by my dismissive cut down, but instead he laughed. "You know, Tisha, that's why I like you. You're stubborn, some would say a challenge. You're probably used to men who shy away from opposition. But me, I appreciate a little resistance, the whole playing hard to get role."

"Nobody's playing," I snapped at him.

"We'll see," he said, not demonstrating the least bit of worry.

"You think so highly of yourself, don't you?" I mocked him, trying to penetrate his cool demeanor.

He shrugged. "So do you. What's wrong with that?"

I twisted my lips, incensed. "I'm nothing like you."

He leaned in closer to me. I could smell his cologne—reminded me of Amani, but it was probably a knock-off. "Dream on, sweetheart," he said in a low voice. "We're more alike than you think. And the parts of us that are different, only make the connection between us stronger."

I sucked my teeth. "Connection? There's *no* connection."

He grinned and leaned back away from me. "Like I said, we'll see."

The captain announced that we were allowed to play approved electronic devices. Aggravated by my row-mate, I pushed my ear pods into the canals of my ears and turned my iPod all the way up. I couldn't stop the man from winking at me and letting his eyes roam over my body, but I could tune him out and pretend he wasn't there. Of all the people in the world to get stuck next to for four plus hours, it had to be this guy—a ridiculous excuse for a man. There was no way I was dealing with this kind of obnoxious behavior for my entire vacation, and I definitely had no intentions of sitting next to him on the flight home. I made two mental notes: one, to change my seat for the return flight, even if I had to pay an additional fee to get upgraded to business class, and two, to chew Amber and Eric out the moment we got off the plane. They were sitting several rows in front of us in business class, too far away for me to get their attention at that moment. But as soon as we got to Vegas, it was on like popcorn.

Taking my frustration out on my magazines, I flipped through the pages aggressively, finding no solace in the superficial articles. If my plane experience was any indication of what to expect for the entire trip, I was ready to turn around and go back home. I needed relaxation and enjoyable activities to get my mind off my plummeting career. Amber had promised me fun and I was going to have fun by any means necessary—even if I had to paint the entire Las Vegas Strip red.

Lesson 5: Joy and Pain, Sunshine and Rain

That ye may be the children of your Father which is in
heaven: for he maketh his sun to rise on the evil and on the
good, and sendeth rain on the just and on the unjust.
(Matthew 5:45)

Nelson

I felt like I had died and gone to heaven. The Vegas trip was
exactly what I needed after the death of Charmaine. For
weeks, I walked around feeling as if someone had sucker
punched me. I could barely sleep, I'd lost my appetite; come to
think about it, I wasn't even trolling for women anymore. I
never realized how much I still loved her until the day she
called me with that horrific news. Behind all of the resentment
I harbored towards her were those same feelings I had 25 years
ago. I'd suppressed them, but they had never gone away.

After about a month of mopping around, I started to get
excited about going to Sin City. Surely there would be enough
trouble to get into in Vegas to cleanse me of all of my sorrow.
I'd overslept the morning of the flight and found myself
rushing to the airport. God must have been on my side
because not only did I make it to the gate in time, but my
assigned seat was next to Amber's friend Tisha. The woman
was so hot it burned my eyes to look at her for too long. It
wasn't that she had the best shape or the cutest face I'd ever
seen—I've dated many models who were way more attractive

than Tisha—but I found myself turned on by her high level of confidence and take no prisoners attitude. I was tired of women with low self-esteem who only wanted a man to make them feel secure about themselves. I was more impressed by a woman who knew her worth and wasn't afraid to demand the best from a man. I saw a lot of Charmaine in Tisha. You could say their personalities were similar, even though I wasn't trying to recreate my relationship with my ex by flirting with Tisha. If someone asked me about my preference in woman, I'd have to admit that if I were to ever get serious again and monogamously date someone, it would be a lady like Tisha—but I had no plans to give up my player card anytime soon. I simply found it entertaining to get a rise out of her.

After pestering Tisha for the entire duration of the flight, I stepped off the plane to see the most amazing site—slot machines in the airport! I'd been to Las Vegas a few times before, but with each trip, I was always surprised to see such an unconventional airport. It was like the city needed for you to go home penniless. And just in case you made it back to the airport with a few coins jingling in your pocket, McCarran's slot machines would rob you blind of whatever was left. I absolutely loved a city that was so unscrupulous. Anything was possible in the state of Nevada. If it wasn't really a desert and so far from my family, I'd probably relocate there to be able to experience that kind of lifestyle on a daily basis.

The four of us walked through Terminal 1, heading toward baggage claim. It took everything in me not to drop a dollar or two into the colorfully lit machines, but I knew I'd have plenty of time to lose my money once we got to the hotel. If Eric thought I was going to be on good behavior since I was technically there for a church-related event, he had another thought coming. I was going to milk this trip for everything I could, singles conference or not.

We retrieved our luggage and proceeded to ground transportation. Though I wasn't Amber's biggest fan, one thing I loved about the woman was that she did everything with style. My brother couldn't have picked a better wife if he wanted someone who was going to upgrade him. Amber had arranged for us to be picked up by a limousine and driven to our hotel. It was so cool when we walked up to the chauffeur who was holding up a sign that read HAYES, and he immediately gestured for a couple of skycaps to help load our bags into the trunk while he escorted us to the back door and held it open.

The limo was equipped with a surround sound stereo system and a mini-bar—bottled water and champagne sitting on ice for us. Eric and Amber grabbed the water while Tisha and I took advantage of the bubbly. The host hotel—the MGM Grand—was only about five or so miles away, but during that brief ride, I turned up the radio and we arrived like celebrities.

Lesson 6: An Unexpected Friend

A friend loveth at all times, and a brother is born for adversity. (Proverbs 17:17)

Lena

"Whoa!" It was all I could say when I walked into my hotel room at the MGM Grand. The room was to die for, but my "whoa" was double-sided. On one side, I had just entered the most beautiful hotel room I'd ever seen. The online images of the hotel and casino were immaculate and I imagined the rooms would be nice, but seeing it in real life exceeded all of my expectations. The walls were beige with plumb-colored paintings. The carpet was also beige with large, chocolate splatter-like designs. There were two queen sized beds against the right wall. Wooden headboards were attached to the wall and accented with stuffed, plumb-colored fabric stretching upward from the beds to the ceiling. Mirrored glass panels surrounded each headboard, giving the room an elongated look. The room was complete with a 40″ flat screen TV, cozy, plum and sliver club chairs, mini bar, a glass top executive desk, huge windows with an awesome view of The Strip, and the bathroom contained the fluffiest white towels I've ever seen. From that point on, my dreams of heaven would resemble this hotel room.

The other side of my "whoa" wasn't as pleasant. I had a roommate. I knew the conference would be pairing us with another attendee of our same gender, but entering the room to find another woman had first pick of the beds rubbed me the wrong way. She was lounging on the bed closest to the window—the one I would have picked had I'd gotten there first—watching a reality show on TV. When I stepped into the room and rested my larger piece of luggage on the remaining bed, she slid off the bed, muted the TV, and approached me with the remote still in her hand.

"You must be Lena Henry!" she squeaked. "Hi, I'm Jessica Olsen. Is this room cool or what?"

She was too peppy for my tastes. Not wanting to rain on her parade, I swallowed a smart remark and said, "It's very nice. I guess we're roommates for the next several days."

She smiled brightly. "Yep. I'm so amped about this conference. I know it's going to be exactly what I need. Las Vegas is so wonderful. Aren't you excited?"

Nope, not really, I thought, especially if I was stuck with her high-pitched voice for the entire stay. How could I be in the hotel room of my dreams with Minnie Mouse?

She was looking at me with anticipation, waiting for me to tell her I was just as excited as she was. I couldn't do it. "I'm glad to be in Vegas, but I'm not so sure about this conference."

She tossed the remote control onto her bed. *Was she going to try to hoard the remote all five days?*

"Why not? There are going to be singles from all over the country here. Have you seen the schedule? There's so much going on, I don't know where to start."

I sat down on my bed, still holding on to my carry-on bag. I had walked into the room less than three minutes prior and I was already bored by our conversation. "What schedule?"

"Did you go by the registration table?"

"No, I just checked in at the front desk."

"Well, put your bag down and I'll show you where to sign in. They'll give you a tote that has a bunch of goodies and the schedule. There are different workshops going on throughout the day, so we get to pick which ones we want to attend. The

only session that's required for everyone is the Singles 101
class which is held at ten every morning."

Before I could object, I was being led out of the hotel room,
down the elevator, and to the conference area that was
bustling with other attendees. We waited in line for about
fifteen minutes before reaching the check-in table and
retrieving my registration materials. There were so many
people hanging around the conference area that we decided to
take a seat in a couple of nearby chairs and observe the other
conferees. While we sat, I pulled the schedule out of my bag
and began perusing the various workshops. Although a few of
the sessions seemed too religious for me—like *Exploring Your
Spiritual Gifts*—other workshops didn't sound too bad—such
as *Always a Bridesmaid*. I wrinkled my nose and let out an
audible grunt when I noticed the classes Eric and Amber were
instructing.

"What's wrong?" Jessica asked.

"Nothing."

"You don't like any of the workshops?" Her voice was still
irritating, but I appreciated having at least one person at the
conference that I could talk to.

"No, that's not it. Some of them sound alright. It's just that
. . . my ex-boyfriend and his wife are teaching a couple of
them."

"Really? Did you know they'd be here?"

"Yeah. He's the one that told me about the conference in
the first place."

"So you all still communicate? I don't know if I could be
friends with any of my exes. It would be too painful."

I sighed. Whether I liked it or not, Jessica was determined
to really get to know me. My first inclination was to ignore her,
not wanting to tell a complete stranger anything personal
about myself, but then I considered the alternative—walking
around the conference friendless. Five days was a long time to
be a loner, so I lowered my guard and let her in . . . a little. "It
certainly isn't a walk in the park for me, but we have a

daughter together so it's like we're permanently connected to one another."

"Do you still love him?"

She certainly didn't ask easy questions. I almost choked, but instead I gulped and said, "I don't know."

"You don't know how you feel about him?"

"Of course I still care about him, but he's married now and his wife is little Mrs. Perfect so it really doesn't matter how I feel about him, does it?"

"It matters to you. If you don't love him, why did you agree to come out to Las Vegas with him and his wife for a singles conference that you obviously couldn't care less about?"

"I don't know. I just didn't want him and her having all of the fun while I sat at home miserable." I looked toward the entrance and spotted Eric and Amber in the vicinity, walking in my direction. I felt myself tense, unsure of how awkward it would be to speak to them in front of Jessica, whom I had barely become acquainted with. I didn't want her to make a mistake and ask me something about him while he was within earshot, so I gave her a heads-up about his presence. "Speak of the devil and he will appear. My ex and his wife just walked in. They're headed this way."

"Lena, I see you made it," Eric said as he and Amber stopped in front of us.

"Hey, Lena," Amber greeted me.

"Yeah, I got in town about an hour ago," I said. "This is my roommate, Jessica. Jessica, this is Eric and Amber." I purposely left off the Hayes part. I hated that Amber was now a Hayes—like my daughter—but I wasn't.

Eric and Amber acknowledged Jessica with a hello. "So where are you from, Jessica?" Amber asked.

"Chattanooga, Tennessee."

"Oh wow. You've come just as far as us," Amber said, acting as she cared about Jessica's travels.

"Yes, and I'm so glad I did," Jessica said, giddy. "I can't wait for the conference to get started. Lena tells me that you two are teaching some of the workshops."

Amber nodded. "We sure are. Eric is leading a men's class for single fathers and I'll be facilitating a class on entrepreneurship."

Eric interrupted. "Well ladies, we need to get to a meeting, but it was a pleasure meeting you, Jessica. Hopefully we'll see you around the conference. Keep Lena out of trouble for us."

"I'll try my best," Jessica said.

I offered the both of them a nonchalant head nod before they walked away.

When they were at a distance, I grumbled. "What did he mean, 'Keep Lena out of trouble for us'?" I asked, mocking his voice.

"I think he still cares about what happens to you."

I rolled my eyes. "He sure has a funny way of showing it." In that moment, I began to regret the entire trip. "Tell me the truth. Am I dumb for even caring about what he thinks of me? I probably shouldn't have come to Vegas. I don't know what I was thinking."

Jessica looked at me with compassionate eyes. "No, you're not dumb. I think it's kind of sweet that you still have feelings for him. It's not like you came out here to win him back or anything . . . right?" She giggled.

At least someone found my life amusing. Too bad it wasn't me. I frowned. "What if I did? Would you think I was crazy?"

Realizing I was serious, she stopped laughing and attempted to handle me gently. "No, not crazy, but you're taking a big risk. What if it doesn't work? What if it does? He's married. If he wanted you back, what would happen to his wife? There's a lot to consider. But I'm not judging you. I have my own problems to deal with," she said.

"Really?" I asked in disbelief. There was no way that Miss Optimistic had any real problems. "So, what's your story?"

Her eyes lowered to the ground and her chipper demeanor fell. "I've been with my boyfriend for seven years and he won't propose. We've talked about marriage, but he says he's not ready. That's why I was so excited about coming to this conference. I needed to get away from him and figure out what to do next. Do I leave him? Do I hold on and wait? I'm getting older and I don't want to miss out on having a family because I waited for him, but at the same time, I really love him and can't imagine being with anyone else." When she looked up at me, I could see the tears forming in her yes.

Feeling a little bad that I had prejudged her, I wrapped my arm around her shoulder and gave her a friendly squeeze. "Join the club. Somehow, I think this conference has matched us up as roommates perfectly."

She nodded and I was sure that Jessica and I would be inseparable from that moment on.

Lesson 7: Out of the Frying Pan and Into the Fire

For there is not a just man upon the earth, that doeth good, and sinneth not. (Ecclesiastes 7:20)

Tisha

I thought everything would magically improve the minute I landed in Las Vegas. I was wrong. Nelson "oohed and ahhed" at everything in the airport and along The Strip as we made our way to the hotel, further adding to my aggravation. I kept telling myself that if I could only get to my hotel room, I'd be okay. I could take a nap, watch some TV, order some room service, and pretend that my life was exactly the way I wanted it to be.

We arrived at the hotel and checked into our rooms. Before heading up the elevator to my room, I stopped in the registration area and signed in. My goal was to handle all that needed to be done so that once I got to the room, I wouldn't need to leave it for a while, maybe even the rest of the night. As much as I was ready to explore Vegas, I had a throbbing headache and wanted at least one good night of sleep before the partying commenced.

But that's not what happened.

I entered my room to be greeted by loud music. The video channel on the TV was turned all the way up and my roommate for the conference was singing and dancing to Pharrell Williams' song "Happy."

Well, at least somebody around here was happy, even if it wasn't me.

"Hey, girl!" my roomie screamed the moment she noticed me standing at the entrance of the room with my rolling luggage still attached to my hand. I had not completely stepped all of the way inside the room because I was debating whether or not I should go back downstairs and demand another room. However, the wacky woman had already spotted me, so I decided to at least give it a try with her.

I walked further into the room, closed the door behind me, and pulled my luggage over to the bed closest to the window. I wasn't sure which bed she had selected, but it really didn't matter to me. She hadn't placed any personal items on either bed, so as far as I was concerned, it was my choice. Without discussion, I decided that I was sleeping near the window and that was final.

"Hey," I said after placing my suitcase on top of the bed. "I guess we're roommates, huh?"

She turned the TV down, but only a smidge. "I guess so. I'm Sky Adams from Daytona Beach. And you are?"

"Tisha Dawson. Atlanta."

"Cool. I hope you're ready because we're about to party as if our lives depend on it."

I dug through my purse, found my bottle of ibuprofen, and swallowed two. "I'm all down with having a good time, but not tonight. My head is killing me, and I just need to chill out this evening."

She crossed her arms and shook her head at me. "Are you serious? Do you really want to spend your first night in Las Vegas, Nevada, locked up in the hotel room? I can't let you do that. You've got to come out and celebrate with me."

"Yes, I really want to spend my first night in Vegas in the room. I'm sorry, but I can't do it tonight."

She frowned. "Such a party pooper. It's a shame because you're too young to act like that. How old are you? Twenty-eight? Twenty-nine?"

I plopped down on the bed. "I wish. I won't tell you my real age, but I left my twenties behind a while ago."

"At least you haven't hit your forties yet. After about 45, it's all downhill. My 47th birthday was last month and I'm still celebrating. Got to get my dancing days in while my knees are still in decent shape. For now, I can still *get low* on the dance floor, but in a few more years, I won't be able to get back up." She proceeded to demonstrate the dance, easing her body down to the floor by bending her knees then standing back up. I really didn't need that visual.

"I haven't gotten *low* in a long time," I said. "I can't even remember the last time I've been to a club. My job has me way too busy for all of that. Plus, I'm always a bit nervous that I'm going to run into one of my former students while hanging out. And that definitely won't be a good look."

"Students? Are you a teacher?"

"High school principal. What do you do?"

"Hairstylist. I used to do hair from home, but when my husband got killed overseas several years ago, I started working at a salon, just to get out of the house. Plus, my kids are older now so they don't need me around as much."

I instantly felt sorry for her. I made a mental note to be nice to her. She probably was still in mourning. "You're a widow? Sorry about your husband. Was he in the military?"

"Yeah. Army. Thanks. It was difficult at first, but it's gotten easier over time. I still have my days, you know? Nevertheless, life moves on."

"You said you have children. How old?" I asked.

"My kids are 16, 18, and 21," she said, counting them off on her fingers. "The 21-year-old wanted to come to Vegas with me, but I was like no way! This is momma's time to let loose, find me a man. I'm not about to have my trip ruined worrying about where she's at and who she's with."

I wanted to laugh, but I didn't want to offend her. "I see. Good luck with the whole finding a man thing."

"You must have a boyfriend back home."

I quickly shook my head. "Actually, I don't. I really don't have time for relationships. I keep a few men around to entertain me, but I'm not interested in anything serious."

"That's always when it happens," Sky said.

"When what happens?" I asked, not following her train of thought.

"You always find the one when you least expect it, when you aren't looking for it. That's how I met my husband. I was at the mall, shopping for a dress for my senior prom and he stopped me and asked me out. I went to the prom with another guy, but soon after, the guy and I broke up and my husband swooped in. Ended up married two years later. You have to be careful of the ones that pop up when you're least expecting it."

I was about to refute her idea, but was halted when I heard a knock at our door.

Sky sauntered over to the door and opened it while I laid down on the bed and closed my eyes. "Las Vegas does not disappoint. Please tell me that you come with the room," I heard her say.

I peeked over at the door and watched Nelson grin at her as he entered the room.

"Technically, I don't come with the room, but I can move in if you'd like," he said smoothly to Sky.

She scanned him as if he were fresh cut steaks at the meat market. "Aren't you a cutie? If you go get your bags, I'll have the concierge make you a key," she flirted back.

"Why me?" I groaned.

Nelson turned his attention away from Sky and made his way over to me. "I guess I came to the right room. Tisha, you didn't tell me that your room was the official party spot," he said as he sat down at the edge of my bed. The TV was still blasting videos—Prince's "1999" now playing.

I rolled my eyes at him. "What do you want, Nelson? Haven't we seen enough of each other today?"

He laughed. "Seen enough of each other? Baby, that's impossible."

Sky finally turned the TV all of the way down. "So you all know each other?"

"Unfortunately. Sky this is Nelson. Nelson is my best friend's husband's brother. He's also annoying and a washed up player. Did I leave anything out, Nelson?"

"Yep," Nelson said, winking at me. "The part about you being my future baby's mother."

"I like him, Tisha. Can we take him with us?" Sky asked.

"Take me where?" Nelson inquired.

"Out to a party tonight," Sky said.

"I'm not going out," I reminded her.

"Yes, you are," she countered.

"I'm coming for sure!" Nelson said.

"No, I'm not," I contested.

"Can my roommate come, too?" Nelson asked. "He seems like a decent dude. At least I'll have one man to hang with since I'm sure Eric won't be able to spend two seconds away from Amber."

"Who's Eric and Amber?" Sky questioned.

I jumped up from the bed. "Would the both of you stop? Sky, I'm not going out tonight. I already told you that I need to rest. Nelson, when I do decide to go out, it won't be with you, around you, or nowhere near you. I don't care if your roommate goes because I won't be there. Have I made myself clear?"

Less than two hours later, Sky, Nelson, Nelson's roommate, Owen, and I walked into Tao Beach, an outdoor pool club at the Venetian Hotel.

Nelson

I made it to my hotel room before my assigned roommate. Getting there first gave me the chance to run around the room like a kid at the playground, exploring every amenity the room offered. I was familiar with every nook and cranny in the room and had begun to unpack when my roommate finally entered.

"Oooh, this is hot!" the man said as he walked in and assessed the place. "How you doin'? I'm Owen Starks."

"I'm good. Nelson Hayes. Yeah, the room is pretty nice," I said coolly, as if I wasn't just as impressed when I first saw the room.

"Forget nice. This room is the truth. See, this is how I should be living every day."

I glanced around and said, "I hear you."

"So where you from?" Owen asked as he claimed the other bed and sat down.

"Atlanta. You?"

"Pittsburg," he said. "A-T-L, huh? You must be a dirty bird fan?" he asked, referring to the Atlanta Falcons football team.

I grinned. "And you know this, mannn! You about that steel curtain?" I asked, alluding to the Pittsburg Steelers.

"All day."

"Usually I would protest to rooming with a Steelers fan, but since it's off season and neither one of our teams went to the last Super Bowl, I'll make an exception . . . this time."

"Thanks, I appreciate that," he replied sarcastically. "So, any idea on what we can get into tonight? I'm trying to enjoy myself as much as I can before I go back home to the wife."

I flinched. "You're married? I thought this was a conference for singles?"

"Not married yet. We're engaged. We haven't set a wedding date and she's hounding me about it. That's why I came to this conference. I figured before I committed to a date, I needed to make sure I'm really ready to take that step."

"I'm not trying to be funny, but shouldn't you have figured all of that out before you asked her to marry you?" I asked.

"I technically didn't propose to her."

"So she proposed to you? These women today are going way too far with this women's liberation mess," I said, frowning.

"Right. I'm saying, how are you going to be a feminist, but you want a man? I don't know too many real men that are trying to hear all of that girl power stuff," he said then laughed. "But seriously, no, my lady didn't propose to me either. We were just having a conversation one day and we got on the topic of marriage. After a while it was like, 'We should get married.' Both of us agreed and we started telling people we were going to get married, but I never officially proposed. That was about a year ago and now she's ready to move forward and really have the wedding, but I just want to make sure it's right before we start planning anything."

"That makes sense. It's better to deal with any concerns you have now then to get married and have to deal with the unresolved issues later," I said. "About tonight, I'm not sure what's going on. I was getting ready to run down to a friend's room and see what she has planned."

His eyebrows lifted. "Your girlfriend?"

I waved him away. "Nah. My sister-in-law's best friend. She's attractive, but she has too much attitude. I just like to make her mad."

"Sounds as if you like her," he said as if he had me figured out.

I chuckled. If he was thinking of playing matchmaker, he'd have to think again. "I'm too much of a pimp to be interested in Tisha. I can't afford to get my player card revoked."

He looked at me as if unconvinced. "Yeah, yeah. Tell me anything."

"How about we do this? I'll run down to her room and see what's going on while you get settled," I said, changing the subject. "By the time I come back, I should have something set-up for us to get into."

He rubbed his hands together excitedly. "Sounds like a plan to me."

On my way to Tisha's room, I prepared myself for her reluctance to hang out with me. I knew it would be a long shot, but I hoped the fact that she didn't know anyone else at the conference outside of me, Eric, and Amber would motivate her to go along with my plans. Eric and Amber would be busy for the duration of the evening, helping to get everything in order for the official first day of the conference. Based on the various duties they had been assigned to do, I highly doubted they would be available much throughout the event. Tisha and I were basically stuck with each other whether she liked it or not.

Tisha's roommate, Sky, was a trip. I could instantly tell she would be a load of fun and would unknowingly help me to push Tisha's buttons. It was obvious to me that Sky was a cougar—an older woman who liked to prey on younger men. I was certain that she would spend a large portion of her time trying to get close to me, Owen, and any other half-decent looking guy at the conference. But I could handle Sky's advances. Like any other woman at the event, she served to entertain me and boost my ego. Of course, Tisha attempted to avoid going out, but between her wild roommate and I, she was no match. She tried hard to put her foot down, but we over-talked her and nagged her until it was more of a headache not to go than to stay in the room arguing with us.

Since it was Tuesday, many of the popular nightclubs were closed. It seemed, like most cities, Vegas' nightlife really exploded toward the end of the week. After searching around online, we decided to attend a pool party. Some of the hotel clubs offered day clubs and daytime pool clubs. It was similar to partying at night, except the fun shutdown when the sunset and most of the entertainment was outdoors surrounding a pool.

Tao was a trendy Vegas nightclub that offered a pool club during the day called Tao Beach. By 6:30 p.m., my new crew and I were dressed in swimwear, with drinks in our hands, dancing to a mixture of House music and Hip Hop. Despite Tisha's protesting, she appeared to be having as much fun as the rest of us. Sky and Tisha danced near each other like women tend to do—I'm not sure why. Owen didn't move around much, he just bopped his head to the beat and raised his hand in the air from time to time. Personally, I came to party, so when invited by different women to dance, I two-stepped my way into the middle of the dance area which encircled the pool. Some people tried to dance inside the pool, but if you've ever tried to even walk in water, you know aqua movement is super slow. After a while, those people gave up and either got out of the pool to dance or simply waved their hands and arms to the tempo.

I was having a blast until I noticed one particular guy dancing with Tisha during a few songs. Just in case you don't know, the man code is as such: a man can dance with any woman for one song and no one will think twice about it. But if he lingers and keeps dancing with the same woman for two or more songs in a row, he's definitely trying to make a connection with that woman. It's like he's marking his territory, sort of like a dog. Several songs with the same woman indicates he's claimed her and is trying to at least stick with her for the night.

By the time I noticed Tisha's situation, I had already danced with at least a dozen women myself. Yet each dance lasted only for one to one and a half songs. I didn't want any woman at Tao thinking that I would be her new beau. When the fourth song commenced and Tisha was still with the same guy, I glanced over at Owen who must have also noticed the same thing because he gave me a you-better-go-get-your-girl look. I excused myself from the cutie I was grooving with and headed in Tisha's direction. The entire way over to her—which was only about a forty-five second walk, snaking my way through the crowd—I'd brainstormed my approach. I couldn't act like I owned her or like she was my girl because Tisha would have picked up on the possessive vibe and called me out. I could already hear her sassy voice in my head. "Get off me. You're not my man!" No, with Tisha I would have to use a different approach. I would have to cancel everyone's fun and call it a night for the entire group.

As I neared her, I reached out and tugged gently on her arm. The guy spotted me and shot me a "Mine!" expression. I ignored his nonverbal cue and said to Tisha, "Come on. We're going to leave."

"Why?" she questioned me. I was hoping that she would just follow my lead, but then again, submission is not in Tisha's DNA. I had to think quickly on my feet before she started a scene.

"The sun is starting to go down. They'll probably be closing the place soon. We're going to go grab something to eat," I said in her ear.

The guy must have felt disrespected because he chimed in. "Hey, dude. Would you mind? I'm trying to dance with the lady."

Tisha stopped dancing and glanced back and forth between her dance partner and me. I guess she realized that the situation could easily become problematic because she said, "Alright, Nelson. Give me a second. I'm coming."

I wanted to pull her away at that moment, but I couldn't risk looking like a fool when she had basically just told me to walk away. Regrettably, I nodded at her and stepped back from her, giving her space to deal with her dance partner. The two of them spoke back and forth to each other, and I watched him pass her a business card before she finally waved goodbye to him and headed toward me. I didn't know why it bothered me so much to witness their exchange. It's not like I hadn't collected a few phone numbers myself from the party. Yet for some strange reason, I wanted to snatch his card out of her hand and rip it into shreds, flinging the debris into the Tao pool.

Owen, being a superb wingman, had pulled Sky away from a 20-something year old man, and the two of them were waiting near the exit for Tisha and me. When we caught up with them, I continued to cover my tracks and said, "Where are we going to eat?" as if it was always the plan.

"There's a Wolf Gang Puck at the hotel," Owen suggested, quickly catching on to my game.

"I'm fine with whatever," Sky said.

"That's cool," Tisha said. "That way I can change, eat, then go to sleep."

"Then I guess that settles it. Let's head back to the hotel," I concluded.

Lesson 8: Count It All Joy

My brethren, count it all joy when ye fall into diverse
temptations. (James 1:2)

Lena

Jessica and I hung out at the MGM Grand that first evening.
We had dinner at MGM Grand's Buffet which I felt was way
overpriced for a buffet. I've been to Golden Corral plenty of
times and I've never paid $29.99 plus tax. The food was good,
but not $30 plus good. I had only been in Vegas one day and
it was eating a hole in my pocket. Luckily, the conference had
given us a boatload of coupons to eat at various restaurants
around the city and there were less expensive options like
McDonald's and Denny's along The Strip. Jessica and I both
agreed that starting Wednesday, we'd be eating more cost
effectively from that point on.

After dinner, we strolled around the casino and I tried my
hand at gambling for a bit. I had a little beginner's luck at first
and won $20. Unfortunately, I kept dumping quarters in the
slot machines and ended up losing the $20 I'd won as well as
an additional $30. Jessica didn't gamble, so by the time she
realized that I was down $50, she talked me off the machines.
I let her convince me, but I had made up my mind that I would
return to win my money back.

We ended up back in our room by 9:00 p.m. and decided
to call it a night. I was still slightly jet lagged, so I welcomed a

hot shower and the cozy white sheets of my queen sized bed. Before I closed my eyes and dozed off, I called Jonelle on her cell phone and checked to see how things were going over her grandparents. She reported that she was enjoying herself, but that she missed me and her father already. It made me feel a little sad that I was so far away from her and couldn't kiss her goodbye. I blew her a phone kiss—making the kissing sound over the phone—and wished her sweet dreams.

On Wednesday morning, I woke up feeling refreshed. I wasn't too keen about having to go to the Singles 101 class every day, but after ordering a light breakfast from room service and eating in bed, I was ready to get the first class over with and enjoy the rest of my day.

All of the registrants piled into a large ballroom with a platform stage and hundreds of seats. After Jessica and I checked in and found a seat, I spotted Eric near the front with Amber and a few other official looking people who I assumed were working the event.

At 10:00 a.m., a middle aged man and woman took the stage and commanded the attention of the audience. As the group quieted down, the woman was the first to speak.

"Welcome to the Singles 101 Christian Conference. I am Lydia Woods and my husband, Martin Woods, and I are your hosts for this exciting event. Over the past five years, we've been offering faith-based courses and retreats aimed at helping people grow in their personal and spiritual relationships. Most of our work has been geared at marriage preparation and enrichment; however, a couple of years ago, we felt the need to expand our training to include resources tailored for single living. This conference is the result of that expansion, and we are delighted to have over two-hundred attendees from all over the United States here with us today. Please give yourselves a round of applause."

The crowd broke out into applause and cheers.

The man, Martin, switched places with the woman during the applause and when the room had quieted again, he began to speak. "The fact that you've taken time out of your schedules and sacrificed money that you could have used elsewhere just to be here with us says a lot about you. It says that you want more for yourself and are willing to do the work necessary to become a better person. We believe that God has amazing things in store for all of you, and that by the time this conference ends, many of you will witness magnificent changes in your life. So let's get started by first answering the question that many of you are pondering. Why did we choose Las Vegas, Nevada as the location for our singles conference?"

He took a breath and continued. "About a year and a half ago, we hosted a marriage retreat on South Beach, Miami, Florida. Even to us, the idea sounded crazy, but following the guidance of the Holy Spirit, we took a small group of married couples to the beach to enhance their marriages. We were astounded by how God used an unlikely place to transform the relationships of the couples that attended. When we started organizing this singles conference, we again had the dilemma of where to hold it. Once again, God pointed us to one of the most unorthodox places to have a faith-based event—Las Vegas. We've come to realize that hosting our events in unconventional places accomplishes three important goals. One, it glorifies God by allowing the participants to experience Him move in their lives despite the circumstances surrounding them. Two, it challenges the participants to remain focused on their personal and spiritual goals in the midst of chaos and temptation. And three, it demonstrates how God can take the most unlikely place and use it for His purpose. There are no limitations to God, and we believe that our events prove the greatness of God by removing our false sense of control and allowing Him to decide the outcome.

"What does this mean for you, our conference attendees?" Martin asked. "Having our conference in Las Vegas means that it is up to you to decide which way you will go and whom you will serve. Every desire a person could have can be found in Las Vegas and most of it is legal. Vegas has a way of making a person feel as if they are on top of the world or living in a fantasy. Everything is big here—the lights, the sounds, the casinos. You could get lost here, not just physically, but mentally and spiritually. We have created a schedule filled with workshops and activities, enough to fill your days and nights with positive, spirit-building opportunities. Nevertheless, you are not obligated to attend any of these activities. You might decide to forego our agenda and create your own, engaging in the allure of Vegas' many attractions. Either way, the choice is yours and we won't judge you. But you must keep these two details in mind. You must attend this Singles 101 class every morning at ten—no exceptions. We don't care how late you stayed out the night prior, you have to be here. We will be checking attendance at the door and anyone who is not accounted for will receive at personal wake-up call from one of our staff members. You don't want this to happen because a personal wake-up call comes complete with a bull horn and ice cold water. Also, keep in mind that you paid for this conference and what you get out of it is what you put into it. If you decide to hang out all day and miss the workshops, you're likely to go back home the same way you came here, continuing on in your same old life. Now, if your life is already perfect, you can afford to miss out on the opportunity we're providing here. But if there is even one area of your life in which you want to see improvement, you need to participate and you need to remain focused."

The woman, Lydia, reclaimed the microphone. "Every day our Singles 101 class will offer insight on two or more biblical verses. It is our hope that by the last day, not only will you have a greater understanding of these verses, but an appreciation and value of how they impact your own life. If you are here, these words are meant for you in one way or another. Your mission is to listen to God and receive what He wants you to know. The Singles 101 class will center on the Book of James, chapter one. If you have your Bible, please turn to

James chapter one, verse two. I will be reading verses two through four."

Shuffling was heard throughout the room as attendees pulled out their Bibles and turned to the specified chapter and verse. I hadn't thought to bring my Bible, but Jessica had brought hers and willingly shared it with me.

"The Amplified version reads, 'Consider it wholly joyful, my brethren, whenever you are enveloped in or encounter trials of any sort or fall into various temptations. Be assured and understand that the trial and proving of your faith brings out endurance and steadfastness and patience. But let endurance and steadfastness and patience have full play and do a thorough work, so that you may be people perfectly and fully developed—with no defects—lacking in nothing,'" Lydia read.

"We thought it fitting for James chapter one to be our focus and theme for this conference, especially as it takes place in a city commonly referred to as Sin City. The theme of this year's conference is 'Count It All Joy.' Many of you may be familiar with James chapter one, but we pray that over the next several days that you embrace and apply these verses to your life. So, let's take a deeper look at what these three verses are actually saying.

"Verse two tells us to be joyful when we find ourselves in tempting situations or in the midst of trials. Your initial reaction to this verse may be confusion. Why should we be glad that we're being tempted to do something we shouldn't or be happy that we are in the middle of a difficult situation? I can speak for myself; I feel great when everything in my life is going well. The moment I find myself in a stressful situation, I no longer feel so good. Matter of fact, I probably feel the opposite of joyful. I feel sad, disappointed, frustrated, and maybe even mad. I start asking questions like: Why me? What's going on? Who did this to me? I have never been in the midst of a trial and thought to myself, 'Yeah, this is good. I like this. Keep the temptation coming. Don't stop the hard times. Pour some more misery down on me.' No, that has never been my response and unless you have some serious mental health issues, it probably isn't your experience either," Lydia said.

The crowd laughed. I sure knew that I wasn't asking for any more misery in my life. I could barely deal with the sorrow I already had.

"But verse two tells us to find a sense of delight in our difficult circumstances. You have to keep reading to understand the rationale behind verse two. Verses three and four explains the reason why. When you go through trials it forces you to use your faith. And the use of your faith produces patience. Other words for patience are steadfastness and endurance. And if you allow patience to develop completely in your life, you will never again feel as if you are lacking or wanting something that you don't or can't have," she said.

"My husband and I love to use examples, so I am going to give you two examples to help you all relate to this point. Since this is a singles conference, I will use one of the big issues that many single people have today—not being married. Let's say your boyfriend breaks up with you and you all have been dating for a few years. You thought he was the one that you would marry, and now you're all torn up because you're getting older, your biological clock is ticking, and now, you no longer have a potential man to marry. So, you're feeling horrible and crying to your friends about how men are all dogs and nobody loves you and you're going to die an old maid."

I could certainly relate to feeling like that. I already felt like an old maid and I hadn't even turned the big 4-0 yet.

"But according to verses two through four, you should see this as an opportunity," Lydia continued. "Yes, your disappointments are an opportunity. So instead of having a pity party, you say, 'Nope, I'm not going to be depressed, I'm going to have joy.' And you put your head up and decide that even though it hurts to get over this guy, you're going to trust God and keep moving forward with your life. You're not worried about the fact that your 40th birthday just passed. You're not tripping about your reproductive cycle and whether or not you still have enough time to have babies. You activate your faith and believe that God knows the desires of your heart, and that in His time and according to His will, you'll meet and marry the man He has for you.

"Instead of running to the club in your catch-a-man outfit, you wait. Instead of signing up for every online dating forum and speed dating event, you chill out. Instead of throwing yourself at every man that comes within two feet of you, you relax. And while you're waiting, and chilling out, and relaxing, patience is being developed in you. You're not anxious about a husband anymore. You can endure another year of being single. You don't flip out when one of your friends gets engaged. Patience is at work in your life, and if you continue to trust God and wait on Him, one day when that good man finally comes along, you're cool about it. You're not messing the relationship up acting all desperate and crazy. This good man is attracted to you because you are complete, whole, and lacking nothing, all due to you letting patience have its way in your life. Are you all following me?"

The crowd yelled out an enthusiastic "Yeah!"

"Awesome. Let's try another example," she continued. "You've been working for a company for ten years and one day, the company goes out of business. You feel distraught. The economy isn't good and finding another job that pays as well as your old job seems impossible. You can only get unemployment benefits for so long, but the amount you receive is pennies in comparison to what you were making prior to the job loss. Maybe you don't have a college degree and trying to get the same level position is difficult because companies now require a degree for that position or you're competing with applicants that have graduated from college. You've got bills to pay, and you're quickly getting behind on your car note, rent, or mortgage. What do you do?

"The Bible says count it all joy, so instead of robbing a bank or getting involved in shady ways of making money, you decide to be positive and give the situation to God. You pray about your circumstances and believe that somehow, some way, the Lord will work things out for your good. While you're waiting for God to come through for you, you continuously send out your resume and go on job interviews. You've got some free time since you're not working, so you enroll in college or a trade school. You take on an internship or voluntary work to gain some additional experience or skills. When you get a job rejection letter or a past due notice in the mail, you say 'Thank you, Jesus. This is my opportunity to trust You.' If they repossess your car or evict your from your apartment, you endure it and continue to praise God. You might even have to accept a low paying job offer temporarily just to stay afloat. But one day, when you finally are working your dream job or running your own successful business, you'll look back and realize that you are in that position because patience was allowed to work in your life and it developed you into a man or woman who is complete, whole, and lacking in nothing. And if one day on your new job or during your entrepreneurship times get hard, you won't get anxious or worried. While everyone else is losing their minds, you'll be relaxed and calm because endurance and steadfastness is already a part of you, and you already know that God will see you through any crisis that comes your way, just as He's done before," Lydia said.

"Amen," was said by various attendees around the room.

"Don't you want to have a life that is stress-free, not because trials don't exist, but because you don't respond to your trials with stress? You respond to them with joy. You get excited because you know that if hard times are present, God is getting ready to develop your character more and take you to the next level in Him.

"Being single is about serving God and allowing Him to prepare you for the future He has for you. First Corinthians chapter seven, verse 32 states, 'He that is unmarried careth for the things that belong to the Lord, how he may please the Lord.' Verse 34 says, 'The unmarried woman careth for the things of the Lord, that she may be holy both in body and spirit.' Singlehood is a time to submit yourself to God, to allow Him to use you and mold you in preparation of what's to come. If you do not allow yourselves to be prepared during this time of your life, when you enter into the next phase, you are likely to make a lot of unnecessary errors because you didn't get the proper training. We've all been to a store or restaurant where there is a newer employee who has not been properly trained for the job. They tend to waste time and resources because they have to do every task multiple times just to get it right. It has a negative impact on the experience of the customers and causes the business to lose money. Do you want to be like that untrained employee when it comes to the great plans God has for your life? Do you want to finally get that husband or wife or job you've always wanted, and then mess it up because you don't have the skills or traits to be effective and successful?"

She made a good point, but I was ready. I'd been ready for marriage for years and I was certain that if God gave me a good husband, I wouldn't mess it up . . . at least not this time.

"We look at the staggering divorce statistics in our country and wonder why so many people can't stay married," Lydia said. "I think it's because they were never qualified to be married in the first place. Faith was never activated and patience never had her way in their lives. Endurance and steadfastness was never produced. So the minute the couple had an argument three nights in a row, the husband or wife said, 'I didn't sign up for this. I can't deal with this. I'm out!' And you know what? He or she is right. They can't deal with it. Patience hasn't been perfected in their lives. She can't tolerate the toilet seat being left up or the way he chews his food. He can't handle her gaining a little weight over the years or the fact that she can't fry chicken like his mother. There's no endurance, no steadfastness, and no patience, so marriages begin to fall apart.

"I send you all on your way today, challenging you to view your trials differently. Most achievements in this world that are valuable don't come easy. To have a baby, a woman must go through nine months of pregnancy and hours of labor. To earn a degree, a student must go through years of studies. Life is a series of processes that we all must endure. If we are diligent and willing, we will emerge from each process better, stronger, and wiser than before. We cannot expect to enjoy the best of this life if we aren't ready to go through difficult experiences from time to time. It's all a part of God's plan to make you the very best you. No matter what you face today, count it all joy. It's for your good, it's for your preparation, and if you allow it, it will lead you closer to your destiny," Lydia concluded.

As much as I hadn't desired to attend the Singles 101 class, it wasn't as bad as I expected. It actually caused me to want to try out a couple of the workshops. As the class ended, I stood up and followed Jessica out the door. I decided at that moment that I would try to be open-minded about the conference. I'd paid my registration fee, at least I could try to get some useful information for my money. *Try* being the key word.

Lesson 9: Know Thyself

Don't you know that you yourselves are God's temple and
that God's Spirit dwells in your midst?
(I Corinthians 3:16, New International Version)

Tisha

The first Singles 101 class was extremely interesting. I walked out of the ballroom considering my attitude toward my trials, especially my current job promotion crisis. If what Lydia said was true, maybe God was using my career drama to help me become a better professional. I couldn't say that I was a patient person. I'd learned to endure uncomfortable situations over the years, but mostly it was for the sake of earning something I wanted badly like a degree or the attention of someone influential. My perseverance had never been about developing my character or becoming a more complete individual. Lydia's message had certainly left me in deep thought, and I made a mental note to take time later in the day to reflect more on it.

Returning to our room after dinner the previous night, Sky and I had reviewed the registration materials and highlighted the workshops we wanted to attend. My girl Amber's session started at 11:15 a.m. on Wednesday, following the Singles 101 class. I wasn't very interested in entrepreneurship, but in support of my bestie, I decided to attend her workshop. Sky was interested in owning her own hair salon one day—an actual building outside of her home where she could employ other stylists—so she agreed to come along with me.

Amber's workshop was held in a smaller meeting room and drew a pretty decent sized crowd. I estimated there were at least fifty or so attendees. In addition to Amber's session, there were two other seminars going on at the same time. One session was on health and nutrition, and the other was on creating a singles ministry. Looking at the schedule, there were three, sixty minute workshops/seminars occurring simultaneously, in four time blocks throughout the day. There were also other activities such as morning prayer, morning aerobic classes, evening game time, and nightly socials. As the Woods had explained, there was always something we could do related to the conference.

I proudly watched my friend stand behind the podium in the front of the room, turn on her PowerPoint presentation, and begin her session.

"Good morning, everyone. My name is Amber Ross-Hayes, and today I will be providing you all with some insight about entrepreneurship. I understand that some of you may be at different points in the process of self-employment, so I will give you some basic information and allow you all to ask questions about your specific concerns.

"I started my first business in my 20's, not too long after I graduated from college. It is a realty company in Atlanta—formally Amber Ross Realty, now Hayes & Ross Realty. My husband now runs the company, and I am supposed to be sort of a silent partner, but you all can tell that I'm not really that silent."

The group laughed.

"I also have two other businesses. I own a child care center and a pastry shop. I am extremely thankful to say that all three of my businesses are successful and thriving, even in a somewhat shaky economy. So, the big question some of you are thinking is how did I do it, and how can you do the same. Right?"

Some of the attendees nodded or grunted in agreement.

"Many of you may think the first step is finding something you love, something you're passionate about. That's what society tells us, right? Find your passion. But I disagree. Yes, you should find your passion, and even more importantly, discover your God-given calling. But successful business ownership has very little to do with passion; it's about hard-work, good business decisions, money, and that little uncontrollable item we like to call God's favor. Fulfilling your calling or embracing your passion does not necessarily mean that you're supposed to run your own company. For example, my best friend is here in the room today. Tisha Dawson, could you please stand?"

I couldn't believe Amber had put me on the spot. I gave her an evil glare as I rose to my feet.

Amber winked at me. "Tisha is a high school principal. We went to college together and were practically attached to the hip. But while I was interested in making money and eventually starting my own business, Tisha was more interested in working her way up in the educational system. As many times as I have tried to get Tisha to start her own school or education-based company, she simply refuses to do so. Tisha is what I call a maintainer. I'll explain exactly what I mean by maintainer in a second. Tisha, you can sit back down. Thanks," Amber said.

I sat down, all fifty or so pairs of eyes looking at me.

Amber continued her seminar. "If Tisha is a maintainer, what does that make me? I am a visionary. What I've noticed is that most people fit into one of these categories: visionaries and maintainers. There are some hybrid people who are both, and if we think about this concept on a continuum, we all may have some level of traits from both sides of the matter. Visionaries are the people who are good at coming up with new and innovative ideas. They're the people who tend to seek out new opportunities and new ways of doing things. They become easily bored with repetition and routine. Visionaries are the kind of people who typically start their own business because they are good at creating new ideas and implementing them.

"Now, based on my definition of visionaries, you all probably are thinking that being a visionary is the preferably role. But that isn't the case. Maintainers are just as important as visionaries, and honestly, if it weren't for maintainers, visionaries would never become successful. The majority of people in this world are maintainers, not visionaries. Maintainers are those who have ideas as well, but theirs aren't as large as visionaries. Maintainers thrive on developing smaller ideas within the large idea of a visionary. Maintainers basically take the big vision created by a visionary and bring it to pass. Maintainers are great with routine and predictability. They feel good about helping others and sharing the spotlight."

As Amber spoke, she clicked her presentation which brought up slides on a big screen behind her. "One of the first steps of entrepreneurship is understanding your strengths and weaknesses. You must know what kind of person you are, a visionary or a maintainer, and you must know how your personality impacts your ability to start and operate a company. The reason many new businesses fold is because the owner has not carefully identified his or her own strengths and weaknesses, playing up to their strengths and developing their weaknesses.

"Let me explain what I'm trying to say. I am a visionary. I'm really good at having new ideas and knowing how to build upon an idea. I'm great at networking and figuring out how to obtain the resources I need to put my plans together. But I can't stand doing the same thing every day or even being in the same place. I'm a mommy to a toddler and although I love my child, I hate being home almost every day. I also don't care much for busy work and small projects. My attention span can be short at times, so I need either a lot of excitement or activities that don't require a lot of time all at once to complete. I also don't have a lot of patience, and I can be very aggressive and assertive in professional situations. Knowing all of these characteristics about my personality has helped me to define my job role to best suit me, as well as not to hinder my business progression. Since I know myself, once I create a business, I work hard at finding the right staff to run the business because my personality will kill my companies. Like I told you all, I'm great at ideas and big projects, bad at daily routine and maintenance. For me, finding qualified, highly trustworthy employees is essential to my success. If I try to do it all myself, I probably will burn myself out and run all of my customers away. Now, depending on the kind of business you have and your finances, you might not be in a position to hire staff, but if you are like me, you need to begin planning toward being in a better place where you can get maintainer-like help."

Amber clicked onto another slide. "The opposite is true as well. If you are really a maintainer, but you have a business idea, you may want to enlist the help of a visionary—someone who can take your dream and expand the idea into an executable project. The whole point is that you must begin with understanding who you are and what resources you will need to become an entrepreneur. Often when we talk about resources, we consider material objects. But a resource is anyone and anything that assists you in what you are doing. People are human sources. Money is a financial resource. And God is an all-powerful, spiritual resource."

A guy in the back of the room raised his hand, and Amber acknowledged him. "How do we figure out our strengths and weaknesses? Is there an assessment tool that we can use for business?" he asked.

"There are a zillion assessment tools out there to help you explore your personality," Amber answered. "The most popular one is the Myers Briggs Type Indicator or MBTI which is a personality test that examines your combined personality style and recommends careers based on your results. Many career centers use the MBTI to help people select career choices. You may also consider working with a career counselor to identify your assets. I also recommend a lot of praying, considering your spiritual gifts or taking a spiritual gifts inventory, and talking to your friends, coworkers, and supervisors about how they perceive you. You can actually learn a lot about yourself from what others have noticed about you."

The man appeared satisfied with her response, so Amber continued. "Another vital consideration for new entrepreneurs is overhead. When you are considering starting a business, you need to create a business plan. A business plan is like drawing a map. You are essentially showing yourself and others how you plan to get from where you are to a successful point in your business. In the plan you should have a budget, and your expenses are thought of as overhead. Overhead is the amount you must spend to keep the business going, and it must be subtracted from your capital—your start-up money—and revenue.

"A common mistake new business owners, and even some established business owners, make is having too much overhead. They spend too much money out on things like advertising, employees, decorating their offices, office space itself, office supplies, client expenses, the product or service, etc. Look at it like this, if your company's revenue is $5,000 per month, you can't afford to spend out $10,000 in expenses. You have to control your expenses so that you can actually make a profit. Yes, it usually takes two or more years in business before profits are earned, but the higher your overhead, the longer it will take to get out of the red, referring to being in debt or spending more than you make. Don't spend caviar money when you only have tuna income. Look for ways to save, cut costs, and start small. The more your business grows, you can slowly start to expand into the company you desire it to be. Does that make sense?"

The group responded favorably, and Amber continued on to tell us more about business ownership from working with partners to the importance of handling taxes correctly. Listening to her speak caused me to completely nix the idea of creating my own charter school. Yes, I probably could run my own school very well, but I wasn't interested in having that level of responsibility. Amber gave us a lot to chew on which felt overwhelming to me. Amber was right about me; I was a maintainer. I was much more comfortable with someone else having the big ideas. I was good at helping someone else achieve their goals, which was rewarding for me. I didn't need to be the one getting the ball rolling to feel accomplished.

When the workshop ended a quarter after noon, I hugged my friend and told her how fabulous she was.

"Even though you called me out during the workshop, you did a wonderful job," I said.

"I knew you weren't going to let it go," Amber said then laughed.

"You know I don't mind being in the spotlight, but at least give me a heads up. Then you called me a maintainer. I was ready to fight you at first. But you were right; I am a maintainer. I'd never thought about it before, but I prefer to work for someone else. Your session really helped me narrow down my choices a little more when it comes to the future of my career in education."

"Glad I could help. What are you all up to now?" she asked.

I rubbed my stomach. "I'm starving, so we'll probably go get some food. You want to come?"

"Why not? I'll call Eric and see where he's at, so we can all go and eat," she said while pulling her cell phone out of her purse.

Eric? I rolled my eyes. I don't know why I expected anything different. Married people got on my last nerves.

Lesson 10: What You've Been Looking for Might Be Staring You in the Face

Say not ye, There are yet four months, and *then* cometh harvest? Behold, I say unto you, Lift up your eyes, and look on the fields; for they are white already to harvest.

(John 4:35)

Lena

The first official day of the conference, I kept trying to casually bump into Eric while he was alone. But every time I saw him, he was either with Amber or rushing to his destination so quickly that I couldn't catch up. By dinner, I was feeling disappointed and beginning to regret coming to Vegas for his sake. I hadn't considered that his being on staff might interfere with my access to him.

Later that evening, I was hanging out with Jessica at the conference's game night when I decided to go find a bathroom—well, that's the excuse I gave to Jessica. I was really going out to gamble for a while, but I didn't want to see her disapproving glare. Leaving the conference area, I finally ran into Eric, surprisingly alone and not running as if there was a fire.

"Hey, Eric," I said to get his attention. He was walking in a slightly different direction than I was and I wasn't sure if he'd seen me.

Eric turned his head and made eye contact with me. "Oh, hey. How's it going?" he asked, still walking and not bothering to stop and talk to me.

I chose to change my course and go in his direction. Catching up to him, I said, "Where you headed?"

"I'm going to my room," he said, making a sharp turn toward the elevators.

I hadn't planned to see him at that moment so I wasn't sure of the right thing to say. I opened my mouth and the most idiotic question came tumbling out. "Can I come?"

Luckily, Eric must have thought I was joking because he laughed. "Why would you want to come to my room? Are you having problems with your roommate or something? I wasn't sure how you all would handle being forced to bunk with people you don't know."

I could have kicked myself. Amber was probably in his room waiting for him. I should have asked if he wanted to come to my room. Duh! "No, my roommate's fine. That came out wrong. Do you want to come to my room?"

Eric stopped and looked at me as if I had grown horns. "Why would I come to your room? Are you okay? Have you been drinking?"

"No, I'm not . . . I just thought . . . Ahhh!" I screamed in frustration. "Never mind," I said before shaking my head and miserably stomping away. I had made a complete fool of myself. If he didn't already, Eric certainly thought I was a nutcase now.

Nice job, Lena. Way to make him want you.

Nelson

I was having fun at the singles conference and actually learning something at the same time. The first Singles class wasn't what I expected. With this being a faith-based event, I thought the message was going to be all about how we shouldn't fornicate, drink, or party, or we were going to Hell. Thank God, the Singles 101 class wasn't anything like that at all. It didn't feel like we were being preached to, instead it felt more like the Woods were just talking to us and helping us understand how to make the most out of our lives using the Bible as our guide. I now understood why Eric and Amber were always participating in these courses; it was really practical.

Amber called Eric, who then called me and told me to meet them at the Rainforest Café for lunch. I picked up Owen from our room and we headed to the main floor of the hotel where the restaurant was located. Not too far away from the Rainforest Café was Hakkasan, MGM's nightclub. Passing by the club, Owen and I discussed checking it out on Thursday night when it reopened. When we made it to Rainforest, Tisha and Sky were also with the group, which wasn't a huge surprise considering she was Amber's friend.

Lunch was cool, and afterward we all went our separate ways. Amber and Eric went back to the conference area to help out the Woods. Tisha and Sky decided to walk along The Strip and do some shopping, then go to another workshop later in the afternoon. Owen and I, like typical men, had just ate and were in need of a serious nap.

About 4:00 p.m., Owen and I stopped being lazy and headed outside the hotel to sightsee along The Strip. We explored two nearby casinos, New York, New York and Excalibur. Truthfully speaking, once you saw one hotel, you've really seen them all. Yes, they all had their own unique attractions and décor, but for the most part, they were massive, glorified gambling areas with restaurants and live entertainment.

Normally when I visited Vegas, I gambled some of my money away, but for some strange reason, I wasn't in the mood to place any bets. I threw a few quarters into a slot machine here and there just to say I did, but I didn't concern myself with making money or hitting a jackpot.

It was over 90 degrees outside, and each time we left the sanctity of an air conditioned casino, the desert heat reminded us that Vegas wasn't for the faint of heart. Thousands of people filled the wide sidewalks, going in every direction except home. Aggressive promoters passed out club flyers, coupons, and entertainment booklets to those who they could get to stop moving long enough to receive their handouts. Women marched up and down The Strip in skimpy attire, seeking male attention and hoping to make their trip to Sin City a memorable one. Normally, I'd pull at least one cutie aside and offer to make her day, but my player mojo was off, and not one woman revealing too much skin tempted me to work my magic.

Around 6:00 p.m., we ate at Fat Burger and mapped out our evening. We'd seen information about a murder investigation attraction back at the MGM, so we finished eating and headed back to the hotel. We were walking past the Grand Buffett when we spotted Tisha and Sky leaving out from dinner.

"And we meet again," I said to Tisha as we caught up to them.

"Why me, Lord?" Tisha said, pretending as if she hated to be in my presence. I knew it was all an act, so it didn't bother me one bit.

"Hey, guys!" Sky said, seemingly happy to be around men.

"Where are you all off to?" Owen asked.

"Nowhere in particular," Sky said. "We can't decide if we're going to stay in tonight or go out. Personally, I'm voting for out, but Tisha's playing tired again."

"I am tired," Tisha protested. "We've had a long day today."

"Come on. You're in Vegas. Live a little. You can sleep when you get back to Atlanta," Owen said, stealing my thoughts.

"Whatever, Owen. Where are you two knuckleheads going? Another pool party?"

Tisha's question sounded as if she didn't like the idea of us attending another pool club, but if I recalled, she seemed to have had a great time at the club with us . . . a little too great of a time if you asked me. I wondered if she'd kept that guy's number or threw it out. I was hoping for the latter. "We're on our way to CSI: The Experience," I said. "We'd figured that we'd leave the partying alone until tomorrow night since most of the best spots are closed on Wednesday."

"CSI like the TV show? That sounds fun. Can we come with y'all?" Sky asked.

"Sure thing, but if you all are going to come, don't get in our way. We've got some serious investigating to do and we don't need womenfolk in our way. This is man's work," I said, taunting them.

I knew my tease would get Tisha's naturally competitive juices flowing. Sure enough, she said, "Excuse me? Man's work? Womenfolk? Oh, it's on. Both of y'all better bring your A-game because Sky and I are going to solve the crime before you do."

"They don't know who they're talking to, do they?" Sky asked Tisha, high fiving her in the process.

"Nope," Tisha said, sounding convinced. "But we're about to show them. Come on, boys, and please don't take this butt whoopin' personally."

Owen looked over at me and the two of us burst into laughter. "They think they're going to out-sleuth us? Dream on, ladies," Owen said.

"Don't talk about it, be about it," Tisha said. "Show and tell, my brotha. Let's go."

CSI: The Experience was bananas. It was costly—$28 for each adult—but everything in Vegas had a high price tag. Despite its expensiveness, it was well worth the money. There were three murder scenes with three different killers. We had to investigate the scene for clues, explore what we found in the lab stations, and narrow down the suspects.

I had to admit, the ladies were natural detectives. I finally understood why men frequently got caught cheating. Women were ridiculously observant and nosy. Tisha and Sky were asking questions I hadn't begun to think of. They were touching so much stuff at the crime scene that the people who worked there had to ask them to stop. And they really got into it. You would have thought the two of them were actors on the TV show. Sky was analyzing bullet casings and Tisha was trying to match DNA samples like their names were Agents Dawson and Adams.

They beat us in figuring out the murderer first.

To my defense, my partner, Owen, was too busy texting his fiancée back and forth to pay attention to the evidence. Since we all eventually picked the right suspect, we were given CSI diplomas, which was a nice treat at the end.

After leaving CSI, we strolled down to the West Wing Bar to hang out a little longer. The West Wing Bar was a swanky lounge near the Grand Buffet that played Urban Lounge genre music. The bar had these weird looking, black cushion like seats that extended up the wall then curved and stretched across the ceiling. We huddled together in one of their private coves and ordered their specialty artisanal drinks.

The group discussed everything from relationship and job woes to the singles conference itself. I found myself unintentionally staring at Tisha. She had a lovely smile that lit up her face each time she laughed. She was a mixture of sophisticated and rough around the edges all at once. When she relaxed, she was the coolest chick in the world, but when she was tense or angered, you'd better watch your back. She was extremely focused and she knew what she wanted out of life. She told us about her recent dilemma at work and how she had come to the conference to have space to figure out her next move. I was turned on by the strength, yet slight vulnerability. She was exactly the kind of woman I would take home to my mother, if I ever settled down long enough to do so.

A few times during the night, Tisha caught me checking her out. I could tell it made her feel uncomfortable because each time, she quickly looked away, ordered another drink, or changed the conversation's topic.

By 11:00 p.m., Owen and I walked the ladies to their room then headed back to our own. I took a hot shower and climbed into my bed while Owen spent thirty minutes on the phone talking to his fiancée, Gina. When he finally hung up the line, he sighed exhaustedly and said, "I don't know what I was thinking, coming to Vegas without her."

"What makes you say that?"

He sat back in one of the club chairs near the window. "I can tell by the way she's acting that she's afraid I'm going to hook up with some other girl while I'm here. I wish she wasn't so insecure."

"Have you ever cheated or done anything to make her feel that way?"

"No, she's just always been like that. Some dude before me did a number on her."

"I hate when women dump the last man's issues on the next man," I said. "Not that it's ever happened to me, but my boys complain about that issue all of the time. I never let a woman get that close to me for it to become a problem so I can't personally relate."

He chuckled. "That's because you are like the women who've been hurt. You're insecure too. You just demonstrate it a different way. You don't let anyone else get close."

"I'm not insecure. And you said I don't let anyone get close like it's a bad thing."

"It is! You'll never find the right woman that God made for you if you keep boxing everyone out. Possibly, you've already found her, but you're too guarded to even notice."

"What are you talking about? And who said I wanted to find the right woman? I'm cool with being solo for the rest of my life."

He shook his head as if disappointed. "First of all, I'm talking about Tisha. Second, God said it isn't good for man to be alone. He made companionship for us so that we can live life to the maximum. When you have a good woman by your side, you're able to achieve much more than you could alone. You know how you use your friends as wingmen when you want to get close to a woman?" he asked and waited for me to respond.

"Yeah."

"It's the same idea. Your wife is your lifetime wing-woman. Except she doesn't help you get close to other women, instead she helps you get closer to your personal goals."

I nodded, comprehending his point. "That was kind of real—the thing you just said. You sure you don't need to be teaching one of these workshops? Seems to me that you already know what you plan to do about your girl when you get back home."

"I know that I'm going to marry Gina—she's my world," Owen admitted. "But I just am not sure if we're ready yet. With her insecurity, sometimes she drives me insane. I don't want us to hate each other once we walk down that aisle. Everyone I know who's married says that once you say those vows, the expectation level increases for both parties. She already expects so much from me. I feel like I'm going to constantly let her down because I'm never going to be the perfect man. I'm just me, and I know she loves me, but at times she doesn't accept me for who I am. She's always trying to change me."

I could see that his relationship was very stressful for him, yet despite the work it demanded, I could tell that Owen truly loved his fiancée and wanted it to work between the two of them.

"Man, I give you credit for being willing to put in the work," I said. "For a long time, I really thought women were evil, literally. But when my brother got married and his wife didn't ruin his life, it made me start to realize that all women aren't evil . . . just some of them. If you have one of the good ones, you should do whatever you have to do to make it work with her."

"What about you? What are you going to do, run from relationships the rest of your life?" he asked me.

I sat up in my bed. "I don't know. I came to Vegas because the one woman I ever really loved passed away a couple of months ago. I'd been so resentful about that relationship and how it ended that I couldn't love anyone else. But before Charmaine died—that was her name—she called me and apologized for hurting me and told me that I should let someone love me again. The whole situation tore me apart. I'm still trying to get myself over the pain of losing her. Tisha, she's a cool woman and I do kind of like her, but I'm not sure if I can get serious about someone yet. I'm not ready to trust a woman like that yet."

"I feel you," Owen said. "Just take it slow and talk to God about it. He'll show you what to do and when to do it. And I promise, it won't be as bad as you fear. God has a way of making everything beautiful in His timing."

Lesson 11: Stand Firm with a Single Mind

A double minded man is unstable in all of his way.
(James 1:8)

Tisha

Who would have guessed that I would go to Las Vegas and have a good time hanging around Nelson Hayes? Definitely not me. I was furious when he sat next to me on the airplane. Less than forty-eight hours later, I was running around a crime scene trying to out-sleuth him and laughing at his jokes afterwards while sipping on a drink appropriately called Barely Legal. It was all so unexpected, yet shockingly entertaining.

If we were back in Atlanta, I wouldn't have gone to a place like the West Wing Bar—or any bar for that matter—with him, but after being provoked into going to the CSI attraction with words like womenfolk, I had to spend more time with the guys, if for no other reason than to gloat about solving the mystery correctly before they did. On our way to CSI: The Experience, Nelson put his foot in his mouth when he wagered a bet. The losers had to buy the winners three rounds of drinks immediately after the game. I wasn't a heavy consumer of alcohol, but Sky agreed to it and shook on the bet before I could oppose. When we won, I had to take advantage of spending Nelson's money, so I ordered the most expensive cocktail on the bar menu—three of them.

The next morning, I paid for my gluttony. I moaned in pain as I eased out of the bed and felt a dull thumping inside my skull. I guess that's what I get for drinking during a Christian conference. Who does this stuff? Obviously me.

After praying and asking God for forgiveness for overindulging, and promising myself that I would go easy on the alcohol for the rest of my Vegas trip, I showered, dressed, took a couple of Advil, and went to the second Singles 101 class. I wished it was held outside so I could have worn a pair of shades to hide my reddened eyes. When I entered the ballroom, I attempted to take a seat near the rear of the room so that Amber wouldn't see me. I knew if my best friend who doesn't drink saw me hung-over, I would never hear the end of it.

"I don't want to sit way back here," Sky complained when I took the first available seats I saw.

"Well, I don't want to sit near the front. Do what you want, but I'm staying right here," I countered.

"Hisss!" she said, making a cat like noise, referring to my catty like behavior. "Don't be mad at me because you can't handle your liquor."

I looked around embarrassed. "Could you say that any louder?" I asked sarcastically. "Remember, we are at a Christian event."

"I remember. But you weren't saying that last night when you were turning those drinks up."

"I hate you," I said.

She laughed. "Don't blame me."

"Actually, I should blame you. You're the one that accepted the bet for the drinks."

She cut her eyes at me. "You could have ordered a soda. Instead you were over there drinking scotch like your name's Johnnie Walker . . . So I see you're one of *those* Christians."

"What's one of *those* Christians?" I asked.

"The ones that do their dirt on Saturday then go to church on Sunday trying to act all holy," she answered.

She obviously didn't know Tisha Dawson too well, but in her defense, we'd only met two days ago. "No, I'm not one of *those* Christians, and I'm far from holy acting. I don't even go to church on a regular basis."

Sky appeared confused. "Then what's with all this hiding and pretending this morning?"

She was talking too loud in my opinion, but it might have been me. My head was still pounding, so at that moment, everyone was too loud for my comfort. "For one, I don't want folks judging me. And two, I don't want Amber finding out. She's one of *those* Christians."

Sky took a quick peek around the room. "I see. Well, you might want to duck because she's coming our way now."

I turned my head slightly to see Amber smiling brightly at me while walking quickly towards us. There was no time or place to escape. I was caught red handed like a kid with his hand stuck halfway in the cookie jar.

"Good morning, ladies!" Amber sang.

Her chirpiness annoyed me.

"Good morning," Sky responded.

"Mornin'," I said.

Amber reached over and lifted my chin so she could see my eyes. That morning, I added her to my I-hate-you list.

Amber grunted. "Either you were up all night participating in a prayer-a-thon, or you've been a bad Tisha. Considering there wasn't an all-night prayer-a-thon, I'm left to believe you have a hangover." Amber shook her head in displeasure. "Seriously, Tisha? I know this is Vegas, but you *are* at a faith-based conference."

It aggravated me when Amber got on one of her Holy Roller kicks. She could fuss for hours about nothing at all. "I know, Amber. I didn't mean to have that much to drink, it's just that Nelson—"

"Nelson gave you alcohol? Eric's Nelson?" Amber asked, cutting me off. "Did I miss something? What were you even doing hanging with him? You can't stand him."

"I know, I know. I don't like him, well, I mean . . . I didn't like him. But since we've been in Vegas, I've spent a little time with him and he's not as bad as I thought. But that's not the point. He bet us that he and his roommate could beat us at the CSI game and they lost. And this one over here," I said, motioning at Sky, "agreed to the bet. Winners got three free drinks. I had to buy the most expensive drinks just to rub it in."

Amber shook her head again. "Wait until I tell Eric that you and Nelson are hanging out and getting wasted together."

"It's not like that, Amber," I pleaded, hoping to keep her from getting the wrong idea.

"We'll see, Betty Ford. Anyway, the class is getting ready to start. I hope you're sober enough to pay attention."

"Ha ha. Really funny, Amber. Don't quit your day job," I said.

She rolled her eyes and walked away.

"Now you see why I was hiding," I said to Sky.

Sky nodded and chuckled before the both of us turned our heads to the front of the room.

Martin Woods stood alone at the podium. After leading us in a brief group prayer, he said, "In yesterday's class, my wife spoke with you all about letting patience have its way in your lives. Today, I will cover the next four verses of James chapter one. If you have your Bibles, please turn with me to James chapter one, verse five. We will read verses five through eight."

Neither Sky nor I had brought a Bible to Vegas, so we simply listened as he read the verses.

"The Amplified version reads, 'If any of you is deficient in wisdom, let him ask of the giving God, who gives to everyone liberally and ungrudgingly, without reproaching or faultfinding, and it will be given him. Only it must be in faith that he asks with no wavering—no hesitating, no doubting. For the one who wavers—hesitates, doubts—is like the billowing surge of the sea that is blown hither and thither and tossed by the wind. For truly, let not such a person imagine that he will receive anything he asks for from the Lord, for being as he is a man of two minds—hesitating, dubious, irresolute, he is unstable and unreliable and uncertain about everything he thinks, feel, decides.' Today I want to discuss with you all the importance of being single people who have a single mind," he said.

"I remember when my children were little. Like most kids, they loved Christmas because they were excited about all the new toys they would receive. When they were young, we made them aware that any gifts that appeared under the tree were from us, their parents, and not a jolly, bearded man in a red suit. So each year, our three children would come to us by the first of December and tell us what they wanted for Christmas. Usually, we already had an idea of what they wanted based on what they already had, what was the most popular, new toy, and what they had been talking about throughout the year.

"Well, one year, when my son, Martin Jr., was about 10-years-old, he couldn't decide what he wanted. That year, a bunch of really cool new toys had emerged onto the scene between summer and Thanksgiving, making it hard to narrow down his most desired gift. So he came to me in late November, right before Thanksgiving, and asked for this new, somewhat expensive bicycle. My wife and I agreed to get the bike for him on Black Friday. So we woke up early in the morning and fought through the crowds to get him that bike. We bought the bike and put it away somewhere safe so that we could bring it out on Christmas. Well, a few days later, he came back to me and told me that he no longer liked the way the bike looked because his friend has the bike and he'd seen it up close. He went on to ask for a bunch of action figures instead. Lydia and I were not happy about his change of mind because we'd already gone through all that trouble to get the bike that he suddenly didn't want. But it was Christmastime, so we decided to be nice, and we returned the bike and got the action figures," Martin said.

"Then about two weeks later, he came back to me for the third time, and now he's had a chance to ride his friend's bike, and of course, he wanted the bike again. When I questioned him about the action figures, he told me that they're for little kids and he's too big for them. I was completely frustrated with the child, but I took the issue to my wife. Lydia is usually the patient one out of the two of us, but in this case, she surprised me and told me to take the action figures back, and that Martin Jr. wouldn't get either toy that Christmas. I thought she would change her mind and give in to his request, but she didn't."

Several chuckles were heard from the audience.

Martin paused for a second, then continued. "Christmas day came and Martin Jr. was disappointed to find out that although he did get a few toys, none of them were the bike or the action figures that he said he wanted most. His sisters both got what they asked for which made him even more upset about it. When he asked us about the matter, we sat him down and explained to him that his indecisiveness had caused us too much time and energy. Since he couldn't make a choice and stick with it, we weren't willing to keep running around town trying to please him. In addition, the first time we bought the bike it was on sale. But once we returned it, we could no longer take advantage of the one-day sale price, and we were unwilling to pay more for it because he'd changed his mind again. That Christmas he learned a huge lesson about being double-minded. After that, he waited to tell us what he wanted until he was absolutely sure about his choice. To this day, he tends to be very intentional in his decision making."

The crowd laughed.

"Just as my son experienced at age 10, the Bible tells us to be single-minded in our requests to God," Martin said. "God is a parent who loves us and is willing to give us blessings out of His abundance, but we must ask Him with a single mind. Like me and my wife, God is not going to run back and forth trying to please you when you don't really know what you want.

You'll end up missing out on what He has for you because you won't make up your mind."

Martin looked down at his Bible and notes briefly. "Going back to the verses in James, the Word is teaching us four important lessons. First, if there is something we are lacking, God is able to meet our need. If you remember in the previous verse from yesterday, we were told that if we let patience have its way, we would be complete and lacking nothing. So the message is continuing on to say you don't have to live a life of lack. The process of patience will get you to a place of completion, but it begins with making our request known to God. If you pay closer attention to verse five, it specifically states that if someone is lacking wisdom, that person can ask God for it and He will give it to them. Having wisdom is vital for any decision that you need to make in this life. Should you marry the person you're dating? Should you date that person you just met? Should you relocate to another city? Should you go back to school? Should you apply for a particular job or opportunity? Should you go to a singles conference in Las Vegas? You need God's wisdom to make the right decision in all of these matters. But let me make this clear, the right decision doesn't mean everything will be perfect, it simply means you'll be on the path God wants you to be on, despite any good or bad circumstances that occur along the way."

A few people in the room yelled out, "Amen."

"Second, these verses let us know that God's not mad at you. It says that He gives freely without grudges, reproach, or faultfinding," Martin continued. "When you ask for wisdom from God, He's not going to turn around and say, 'Nah, I'm not going to give him or her any wisdom because the last time I gave that person something, they didn't appreciate it.' If you made a mistake ten years ago, one year ago, yesterday, or even this morning, He's not holding it against you. He's just glad that you came back to Him. He's pleased that you understand that you need His wisdom and direction. He gives it freely so that hopefully, you can make better choices from now on. Like with my son, the next year, my wife and I weren't saying we wouldn't give our son a chance to request another gift because of how he acted the previous year. No. The next year he asked for something else and we gave it to him. We didn't criticize him or hold a grudge against him. We let it go because we love our son. God loves you even more and He's not mad at you.

"Third, the verses reveal to us that it takes faith to receive from God. It says, 'it must be in faith that he asks with no wavering.' Remember in yesterday's lesson, my wife explained that your trials cause you to activate your faith and that 'the proving of your faith' produces patience. Once again, faith is in the middle of the process. It's not enough to just ask God for something like wisdom, you must also believe that He will give it to you. What's the point of asking for something that you don't think you'll receive? Why waste your time and God's time? That's like me going to Burger King and asking for a Big Mac."

The crowd laughed.

"I don't really think I'm going to receive a Big Mac because I know that only McDonald's sells them," Martin said. "Burger King doesn't even have the right ingredients to make a Big Mac correctly. The workers at Burger King might even be offended that you came inside their store and requested their competitor's food. In the same manner, going to God and asking Him for something that you don't think He can give you is an insult. Are you trying to say that He's not God and He doesn't have what it takes to give you what you asked for? Why don't you believe? Why are you wasting His time if you don't think it's possible? Multiple times in the Bible we are reminded that our faith is essential to receiving what we need. You must activate your faith and believe that your request can and will be fulfilled."

Martin looked down at his notes once more. "Fourth, a double-minded person will not receive the request they made to God. The Bible says that a double-minded person is like the sea, being tossed back and forth by the wind. A double-minded person is unreliable, undependable, and cannot be trusted because he or she is always uncertain. Imagine asking someone to pick you up after work and that person says, 'Sure.' Then a few minutes later says, 'I can't.' Then an hour later says, 'Okay, I'll be there.' Then thirty minutes after that says, 'I don't think I can do it.' If you're anything like me, you're going to get upset and say never mind. That person cannot be trusted; that person is too flaky. God feels the same way. He cannot trust a flaky person with His blessings, with His wisdom.

"Let's think of it from the perspective of dating and marriage. You might want to get married, so you ask God for a husband or wife. If you're a flaky person and God gives you a good man or woman who marries you, you might turn around and say you just want to be single again. Then you get a divorce and months later start whining to God about how you're alone and you need a husband or wife again. You don't know what you want and you cannot be trusted. You're out here wasting God's time and hurting people because you can't make up your mind. If you want something from God, you must ask for it in faith—believing that you will receive it—and you must be certain that you really want it and that God can give it to you."

Martin walked from around the podium and closer to the edge of the platform.

"As I wrap up today's lesson, I want you to once again think back to yesterday's message. Using the example of wanting to be married, let's see how this all fits together. We will do this from a female perspective. You're a single woman and you want to be married. So you ask God both for a husband and the wisdom to know if the man in your life is the one you should marry. You believe in faith that God will give you both requests, and sure enough, the person you're dating proposes and God confirms that he's the one you should marry. So you get married and everything is going well until one day, your marriage suffers a major crisis. You husband disappoints you in a big way. Maybe you find out that he lied or cheated or something heartbreaking. Instead of flipping out, you decide to count it all joy and endure your marriage crisis with your head held high, trusting that God will get you through the situation. But the problem isn't resolved overnight, and for six month or a year, you have to continue to deal with this heartbreak. And it's difficult, but you choose to keep trusting God anyway. A year later, when you finally come out of the trial, not only have you survived it, but you've developed endurance and patience. So when you ask God a year later for a child, and three years later for a new house, and five years later for that promotion at work, you have everything you need to not only receive the blessing, but hold on to it no matter what storms may come."

By the time the class was over, my headache had magically disappeared. Martin's lesson had stirred something deep inside of me that I could not deny. I had started to doubt God and what He could accomplish in my life. I was becoming way too dependent on myself which was a slippery slope because I was limited in what I could control. If I was going to overcome my crisis at work, I was going to have to put my situation in God's hands and leave it there, believing that He would work it out for my good. As Martin pointed out, I would have to use my faith and not doubt. The wisdom I was seeking and even the job I wanted were possibilities. God could and would respond to my request, but it was up to me to believe.

Lesson 12: Do the Right Thing

For whosoever will save his life shall lose it; but whosoever shall lose his life for my sake and the gospel's, the same shall save it. (Mark 8:35)

Nelson

The second Singles 101 class was indeed interesting. Single-mindedness. I'd never thought about the consequences of changing my mind or making one decision and sticking with it. In relationships, I'd been a mixture of single and double-minded. I was single-minded about not taking women seriously, yet I was double-minded about who I chose to spend my time with. I would often go out with one woman at the top of the night and end up hanging with a different girl by the end of it. That kind of behavior was acceptable and even encouraged in the players' handbook, but I guess in the Bible it was frowned upon—not that I'm surprised. A lot of my everyday behaviors weren't too Bible friendly.

After the second Singles 101 class, Owen and I decided to attend a couple of the workshops since we'd skipped out on all of them during Day One. Owen wanted to go to a session called What to Do Before Saying I Do, so I agreed to sit with him in that workshop if he would go with me to Eric's Single Fatherhood session after lunch. The What to Do Before Saying I Do seminar was more insightful than I anticipated. Based on the title, I thought it would be a checklist of wedding planning activities, but instead the instructor challenged the group to consider our motives for wanting to be married and to get rid of unrealistic ideas about marriage.

"Marriage is hard work and in order to make it work, you will have to put in the work every day. If you're not willing to give it 100 percent each and every day, you might want to get a hobby or a pet, and forget about finding a lifetime partner," the instructor stated.

Owen was quiet during lunch and I sensed that some of the points made by the session's instructor really hit home for him. I was glad to see him dealing with the issues he came to the conference to address. I didn't ask him whether or not he enjoyed the session; I simply gave him the space to process what had been shared with him.

As advertised, Eric's class was all men, with the exception of Amber who sat in the far back and tried to be inconspicuous.

I knew Eric was the CEO of Amber's realty company, but I'd never really considered him much of a leader. He was my little brother whom I had spent my entire life teasing. It was difficult for me to see him in any other light . . . until that day when I watched him command the attention of thirty or so men.

"My name is Eric Hayes and this is Single Fatherhood," he started. "In the short time I have with you all today, I want to encourage you all to fully embrace your roles as men, heads of households, and fathers. These are not easy shoes to fill, especially for those of you who have not had the best examples of how to play these roles, but with commitment, maturity, and the guidance of God, you can take your rightful place in your homes."

Eric walked from behind the podium and moved closer to the group. "Let me begin by telling you my story. I'm actually married. My wife is the only woman in this room, seated in the back."

Everyone turned around and looked at Amber who shyly waved at the group.

"I've only been married for about five and a half years," Eric continued. "However, I have a daughter who will be 14-years-old in two months. If you really want to know something interesting, the mother of my 14-year-old is also here at the conference. Yep, we are all one big, happy family . . . not."

The men in the room laughed.

"Like many men, I engaged in premarital sex with a woman I was involved with, but wasn't ready to marry. I was young, in my twenties, and I thought I had life all figured out, until the woman told me that she was pregnant. She wanted me to marry her, but I barely knew how to take care of myself. How was I supposed to take care of her and a baby? I'll be honest with you fellas—I freaked out. I made every excuse in the book why I couldn't commit to family life. I really should have thought about all of that before I laid down with her, but that's a different message for a different day.

"This woman who I'd slept with had a beautiful baby with me and like many relationships that start out backwards, we could never get it back together the way God intended. Slowly, we began to fight more and more until one day, we couldn't stand each other. So eventually when the arguments became unbearable, we went our separate ways. But there was still this life, this baby we had created together who was now stuck in the middle of this tense relationship between two people who didn't like one another. Now, I am in no way ashamed of my daughter, and I thank God for her being in my life every day, but I often struggle with the situation in which she was birthed into. I grew up with a mother and father in a traditional, Christian home, but somehow, my sin had led to my daughter being stripped of the basic home environment that I'd been afforded."

Eric walked back to the podium. "That's what sin does; it breaks down relationships. Whether it's the relationship between us and God, between us and our significant others, or us and our children, sin destroys relationships if we allow it in."

I looked at my little brother in admiration. Who knew he could be so intense? Amber and this new ministry he was under was definitely making him a better man.

"So what do you do when relationships have begun to breakdown? You attempt to fix them," Eric said. "Unfortunately, the more you try to make relationships right, often the worse they become. My story is probably very similar to many of you all. We decided to have this particular workshop because a lot of attention, care, and resources are often provided to single mothers, but fathers are frequently denied encouragement, help, and the tools we need as well to take care of our families. Just because some of us aren't in the same home as our children doesn't mean that we don't want to be. Just because sometimes we go unemployed for periods of time doesn't mean that we don't want to provide for our children. Society has to stop blaming us for everything bad that happens within the family, has to stop accusing us of being deadbeats, and we have to start believing in ourselves, that we are worthy of respect, success, and positions of leadership. The Bible says that we are to be revered, that we can be prosperous, and that we are the head. Our identity is in Christ, not what people think about us or say to our faces when they want to tear us down. Are you all with me?"

"Yeah!" the men in the crowd said, empowered.

Eric slowed his pace and calmly said, "I met my wife at work. I actually worked for her. She was this intelligent, gorgeous woman that I really appreciated. Over time, I began to look at her differently, not just as my boss, but also as a friend and someone I was attracted to. Long story short, I married her. But remember, I still had this tumultuous relationship with the mother of my daughter. And of course, marrying someone else was like throwing gas on a fire—the drama escalated from a small kitchen fire to the whole house ablaze. We ended up in court, fighting for custody rights, letting some outside person decide how much time we had with our daughter, which to me is one of the most backwards ideas in the world, but it had to be done. With the grace of God, we were able to work our situation out in the end and split time with our child evenly, but my results are not what the majority of men end up with. Some of us rarely or never get to see our children. It's not fair to the kids to miss out on growing up with a man in their lives because the parents couldn't work through their problems. We have to do better, fellas. We have to step up and demand that we get just as much right and access to our children as women do. Just because you're not married to the mother of your child does not mean you don't have a voice or say. Stop letting the enemy make you feel helpless and hopeless. The Bible says that we are more than conquerors through Christ. Martin talked to us this morning about being double-minded. It's double-minded to say you love your children, but then not fight for them. It's double-minded to sleep with a woman, but then not want to marry her. It's double-minded to have a baby, but then not provide for it. We must have a single mind. We must believe in ourselves and do the right thing. God expects our very best. If the world doesn't see the good within us, that's their loss, but we have to be determined to please God and do what is right in His eyes. Can I get an Amen?" Eric asked.

"Amen!" the men yelled back.

My chest swelled with pride as I offered my baby brother a sincere, "Amen."

Lesson 13: Warning Comes Before Destruction

These things happened as a warning to us, so that we would not crave evil things as they did, or worship idols as some of them did. As the Scriptures say, "The people celebrated with feasting and drinking, and they indulged in pagan revelry." And we must not engage in sexual immorality as some of them did, causing 23,000 of them to die in one day.
(I Corinthians 10:6-8, New Living Translation)

Lena

As much as I enjoyed Jessica's company, a part of me felt like she was holding me back. She was a goody two-shoes, and her almost angelic behavior was cramping my style. I wanted to get out and have fun. I had been in Vegas for three days and hadn't been to one party or club yet. If I knew that I was going to miss out on all of the action, I could have stayed back in Atlanta with my daughter.

Thursday evening, I broke free of Jessica while she attended one of the conference's night time socials. I was determined to go out dancing, but I was a bit nervous about traveling to a club by myself. Back in Atlanta, the rule of thumb was to always go out with at least one friend of the same gender. Since I hadn't made any effort to get to know anyone at the conference, my only female choices were Jessica, Amber, and Tisha—and I wouldn't be caught dead at a party with any of them. My only remaining option was to take the journey solo.

I dressed in a pair of sparkly gold leggings and a black tank top with gold letters that spelled out I'M THAT GIRL. Completing my look with hooped gold earrings and black sandals, I headed to the casino area of MGM to plot out my final destination for the evening. I figured that I'd play the slots for a little and ask around about potential nightclubs. An hour later, I was down $75 and desperately itching to get out of the MGM Grand. One of the weird features of casinos was that they were a twisted maze of walkways, gambling opportunities, and amenities. There were no windows, few doors, and absolutely no clocks. Trying to gauge the time was impossible, and trying to get outside was a task if you weren't familiar with the layout. I'd been studying the casino floor since my arrival and had eventually found a path that would lead me out to Las Vegas Boulevard.

Tired of losing money, I escaped the clutches of the MGM and found myself standing outside, breathing in the desert air. I walked around the building to the main hotel entrance, figuring I could catch a cab to whichever nightclub I settled on. A group of half drunken women, who seemed to be involved in a bachelorette party, pushed past me on the sidewalk. I'd seen them in the hotel several times and was pretty sure that their rooms were down the hallway from mine. If anyone knew where the fun was being had, it certainly would be these women. I quickly decided to attempt to tag along with them.

"Hey, ladies," I said to one who appeared to be the leader. "Is someone getting married?"

"Yep," the leader spat out. "Me!"

"Congrats! Are you all going out to a club or somewhere now to celebrate?"

She side stepped. "Yes, we're going to the best club in Vegas."

"Woooo hooo!" one of her friends screamed out.

A stretched limo pulled up to the curb in front of us and I knew I would have to work fast if I wanted to join in on the festivities.

"I was looking for a place to hang for the night and my roommate's kind of boring. Do you all mind if I tag along to the club with you?"

"Nope," the leader slurred. "The more the merrier."

In hindsight, it was stupid for me to hop inside a limo with a group of women I didn't know, in an unfamiliar city going to a random club, but at the time, it seemed like a good idea. The ladies had more than likely been drinking all day because I could smell the liquor coming out of their pores. One of them passed a CD to the limo driver and they began having a party right there inside of the limo. Being cliché, they opened the moonroof, stuck their heads out, and screamed at pedestrians and other drivers.

After riding down The Strip a bit, the limo stopped in front of a club called Olympic Gardens. The parking lot was packed, so it appeared the women were right—OG was the hot spot. We piled out of our transportation and were led VIP style into the building. After paying a stiff cover charge, we walked into the main bar area and I completely froze.

Olympic Gardens wasn't a nightclub, it was a strip club!

Topless women gyrated for money in front of dozens of lustful men.

"Did you all know this was a strip club?" I tried to ask the leader, but she was too busy heading toward a stairway with her bridal party in tow.

I felt instant relief. At least we weren't planning to stay downstairs in the middle of the ongoing strip tease. Possibly upstairs there was a real night club filled with PG-13 kind of partying. If not that, maybe the women I was with had reserved a private room where they were planning to have their own bash. Either way, anything was better than being downstairs at the OG . . . or so I thought.

We ended up in a large room that served as a second floor bar and lounge area. But I found out the hard way that the OG had not changed its specialty with the change of level; it just altered the pleasure for a different crowd. Barely clothed male strippers flounced around the upstairs area while eager women ogled, danced with, and paid them. I stood at the entrance and stared in horror. It wasn't that I'd never seen male strippers before, but exotic dancing was not the kind of clubbing I was looking for or expecting when I decided to go out.

By the time I got over my initial shock, the bachelorette party had taken over several chairs near the stage and was enticing a man in a cowboy getup over to them with a stack of one dollar bills. I was debating if I should join them despite my reservations when a muscular man wearing nothing but body oil and a G-string moseyed his way over to me and tried to convince me to pay him $20 for a lap dance.

I had to get out of there, immediately.

I nicely turned the dancer down and headed quickly back down the stairs. Rushing through the main floor of the club, I zipped out the entrance and was truly grateful to see several yellow cabs waiting near the door. Hopping into the backseat of one, I rattled off, "MGM Grand."

The cab driver nodded and pulled out of the parking lot. I'd never been so happy to leave a so-called club in my life.

"Did you enjoy yourself?" the cab driver asked.

"Huh?" I asked, realizing he was talking to me.

"Did you enjoy yourself at the OG?"

I grimaced. "No, not at all."

He looked at me through the rear view mirror. "Really? Most women say they love it."

I replayed the scenes from the club. There was nothing to love about it. Why would I want a bunch of sweaty men who I didn't know dirty dancing in front of me? "I guess I'm not most women."

"I hear ya. Everything ain't for everybody. Where you from?"

"Atlanta."

"A-T-L. I've never been there but I plan to go one of these days. What are you in town for? Just vacationing?"

He sure had a lot of questions. What was this? Taxi cab confessions? "No, I'm here for a conference."

"How's it going?" he asked, continuing the interrogation. This guy should get a job as a detective.

Be nice, I told myself. "Not too well. It's okay, but I'm starting to think I shouldn't have come. The conference is providing me with some really good information and advice, but it's just not for me."

"Maybe it is for you, but you're not allowing yourself to embrace it."

"What?"

"No offense. I'm just saying that sometimes it's easy to write off what we don't want to hear. If you came out here expecting one thing and you got something else, you might think the trip has been a waste of time. But possibly the something else is really the reason you were supposed to come in the first place."

It was funny how people who knew nothing about me always felt it was their duty to tell me about myself. He might have made a valid point, but number one, I had not asked for his opinion, and number two, he was irking my nerves by being all up in my business. "That was really deep and confusing all at the same time," I said to him. "Do you talk like this to everyone who gets into your cab?"

"Nope. Only the ones in need of a fresh perspective."

There was nothing wrong with my perspective. Just because I didn't agree with most people around me didn't make my views incorrect. "Well thanks, but if you don't mind, I'd rather ride in silence."

"No problem. We're on your dime."

Tisha

For the third night in a row, Sky and I were hogtied to Nelson and Owen. It was time for me to get over my resistance and accept that these three were my official Vegas crew. I barely saw Amber and Eric, and when I did, they were either rushing to do something for the conference or heading back to their suite, exhausted. To Amber's credit, she invited all of us to her suite on Thursday evening before we hit the night scene. I was stunned that she even spoke to me after seeing me with a hangover that morning, but a few hours later, she called my cell phone and welcomed us to come up at 9:00 p.m.

The fellas met me and Sky at our room and we all ventured up to Amber and Eric's room which was on one of the top floors of the MGM. I knew their room would be extravagant, but I never expected them to be living like they owned the city. Their room was a Skyline Terrace Suite which looked like a two level, one bedroom apartment with an amazing almost 800 square foot outdoor patio. If only Amber and Eric weren't so dull, we could have cancelled all of our clubbing plans and thrown our own party in their suite.

"Are you kidding me?" Nelson yelled as he ran around the suite in awe.

"Make yourself at home," Amber said. "There's some fruit and shrimp out on the terrace."

We all walked through the suite and out onto the patio, marveling at their magnificent view of the Las Vegas Strip.

"I can't believe you all have had such a great room and didn't tell me," I complained.

"I told you we had a suite," Amber responded.

I glared at her. "Amber, a suite is normally a room slightly bigger than the rest with a pullout sofa bed. This is a luxury condo. How can you all afford this room? It has to be well over a thousand dollars a night."

Amber shrugged. "It is a bit expensive, but because of the conference, we got a great deal on the room. Plus, this is our vacation for the year so we decided to splurge a bit."

Eric came out on the patio with a pitcher of water with lemons slices. "Sorry it's not the pretty cocktails you've all been gulping down the last few days, but the wife and I run a dry suite," he joked.

I grimaced at Amber who ignored me.

Nelson poured himself a glass of water and said, "It's not like we expected anything more from you all. We'll make up for this lost time once we get to the club."

"Speak for yourself," I said. "After last night, I'm taking a break."

"Ahh, don't be like that, Tisha. You're much easier to tolerate once you've had a drink or two," Nelson teased.

"That's because after one or two drinks, your face doesn't look so ugly," I shot back.

"Can we have one night without the two of you going at it?" Sky asked. "I swear, you two are like cackling hens."

"Sky, what sounds like cackling to you, is really two people trying to fight their attraction to each other," Owen said.

Eric and Amber gave each other a troublesome look then began glancing back and forth between Nelson and me.

"Owen, why do you have to start with all of that?" I asked, trying to take the focus off me. "Worry about your own relationship. Nelson and I can barely be friends, so romance is completely out of the question."

The patio became uncomfortably quiet. Thankfully, Eric changed the subject. "So what heathen activity do you all have planned for tonight?"

"We're gonna check out Hakkasan. It's the club downstairs," Nelson said.

"You know, the conference is having a karaoke contest tonight. Why don't you all try that out? You don't have to party just because you're in Las Vegas," Amber suggested.

"Amber, please," Nelson said. "None of us came all the way to Vegas to sing karaoke with a bunch of Jesus freaks. No disrespect, but I'm not singing Kirk Franklin tonight unless they play 'Stomp' at the club."

"I hate when the DJ does that. Who really wants to hear a gospel song while they're dancing and drinking at the club?" Sky asked.

Eric laughed. "That's exactly where they need to play some gospel; clear a few of you all off the dance floor. You just hate it because it messes with your conscious."

Nelson waved Eric away. "Don't act like you're so righteous, little brother. I remember the days when you used to shut the party down with your fraternity brothers."

"I did, but those days are long gone," Eric said. "No one wants to party forever, and those who do are just running from responsibility. After a while, we all get tired of going to the same club, hearing the same music, and dancing with the same people who aren't doing anything productive. I'd much rather be at home with my wife and kids."

"Well brother, I don't have a wife or kids, so I'll be at the club," Nelson said then laughed. "And speaking of the club, you all ready to roll out?"

By 10:30 p.m., we were on the dance floor at Hakkasan, jamming to "I Gotta Feeling" by Black Eyed Peas. As much as I was enjoying partying with my Vegas crew, I couldn't help but think about Eric's words. Was having a family the next logical step? Should I be getting bored with the club scene and want more out of my personal life? Was partying unproductive and a way to avoid responsibility?

I wasn't the type to club on a regular basis back home, but I did go out a couple times a month. I had a few other single friends that liked to hang out at age 25 and up venues. We didn't always go to clubs; sometimes we went to music festivals, lounges, or private parties. To me, it was a way to de-stress after a long work week and meet new people. I often met a lot of good looking men at those outings, but never anyone appealing. But maybe therein lied the problem—someone I met out wouldn't be the kind of man appropriate to settle down with.

Not that I wanted to settle down anyway.

The music changed to Lady Gaga's "Poker Face" and I felt someone tug on my hand. I turned quickly to see the guy from Tuesday's pool party at Tao Beach. His name was Larry, and he was in town for a plastic surgery convention being held at the Mirage. Yes, he was a doctor, not that I cared. I'd dated plenty of professional men from doctors to lawyers to accountants. Men were men, and often the more money the made, the more games they played. I loved a man with a fat wallet, but having money didn't automatically mean he was a match for me. He still needed to be attractive and willing to treat me like a queen. So far, Larry was attractive, but I didn't know him well enough to decipher the queen part. He'd given me his phone number, but I'd been so caught up between the conference, scoping out Vegas with Sky, and spending the evenings with the motley crew, that I'd forgotten to call him.

"Larry? Hey!" I said, acting happy to see him.

"I've been waiting for your call," he said.

"I'm sorry. I've just been so busy with the conference. I wasn't avoiding you."

"Well then, I'm glad I bumped into you. Do you want a drink?"

"Uh . . . I . . . I'm not really drinking tonight," I said.

"Come on. One drink with me," he pleaded.

I felt bad that I hadn't called him and he was being so nice. I really didn't want to put any more alcohol in my system, but saying no to him was difficult. "I guess one drink won't hurt. Just one," I said firmly.

"Just one," he promised.

I glanced over at my friends. Owen was doing his usual two-step against the wall. Sky was dancing with a random guy, and Nelson was giving me a disapproving scowl. I looked back at Larry who was waiting for me. Sighing, I nodded and let him usher me away from my crew and toward the closest bar.

Lesson 14: There's Beauty at the Bottom

Let the brother of low degree rejoice in that he is exalted.
(James 1:9)

Nelson

I couldn't believe that Tisha just up and left with that cornball of a guy! Our little group was hanging out at Hakkasan, having a good time, when the dude from Tao Beach showed up out of nowhere. Next thing I knew, Tisha went over to the bar with him. He bought her a drink, which she accepted despite the fact that she kept telling us that she wasn't drinking that night. Then she and the guy started dancing and acting like they were a couple. I lost track of them after a while, but by the time we were ready to go, Tisha was nowhere to be found. Owen and I walked Sky to her room as usual. We all hoped Tisha had just headed back to the room early, but she wasn't there either. Sky started making wisecracks about how Tisha was getting her groove back, but it's not like she ever lost her groove in the first place to have to go and get it back. By the time Owen and I returned to our room, I was highly upset. I was concerned about Tisha's safety and outraged that she would walk out of the club without telling us. She didn't know that guy from a can of paint! How could she go off with him all willy-nilly? There are psychotic people in this world. Why was she acting as if she was never taught "stranger-danger" back in grade school?

Owen tried to calm me down, but I wouldn't hear of it. I wasn't in the mood for his Dr. Phil routine. Instead of listening to him babble, I waited until he went to take a shower, and I left the room. I walked through the casino for a while to air out my thoughts. Yes, I did like Tisha, but I couldn't stand the idea of having feelings for her or any other woman. It was too stressful to care about a woman. We'd only been around each other for a few days and she was already tugging on my emotions. I hated the way I felt, all out-of-control. This was the exact reason why I never put too much of myself into a relationship. Love was unpredictable, and I refused to let some silly woman and her inconsiderate ways cause me to lose my mind.

After walking around aimlessly for an hour, I was about to return to my room when I happened to glance inside of Starbucks and saw Tisha sitting there, having coffee with that lame dude. Without thinking it through, I approached them.

"Where have you been?" I asked, vexed.

Tisha looked up at me and gasped. "Nelson? How did you know I was in here?"

I folded my arms in front of me. "I didn't. No one knew where you were. You just left without saying anything. We were all worried about you. Next time, tell somebody where you're going."

"Okay, Papa," she said, her voice dripping with sarcasm.

"Is there a problem?" her little boyfriend asked.

I ignored the man. "Tisha, let me speak with you for a moment." Before she could refuse, I grabbed her firmly by the wrist and tugged her into the hallway.

She pulled away from me. "What's wrong with you? Why are you acting all overprotective?"

"This isn't a joke, Tisha. We don't know who this guy is and you just disappeared with him."

"I'm sorry, Nelson. I didn't know it was a big deal. You all were having fun, and he asked to go somewhere quiet so that we could talk. I didn't think it was unsafe for me to come over to Starbucks with him," she said.

"You could have at least said something. Don't do that ever again," I said.

She put her hands on her hips. "Who do you think you're talking to? You're not my man. And even if you were, I'm a grown woman."

"Then act like it and stop running off with strange men. Teenage girls do that kind of thoughtless behavior. Grown women demonstrate common sense and self-control."

She sucked her teeth. "Why are you so concerned about what I'm doing? I don't see Sky or Owen down here looking for me. You're the only one who seems to care."

"Maybe that's the problem. Maybe I'm the only one who really cares. I'm going to bed," I said, turning my back on her and walking away.

I sat in the Singles 101 class the next morning unsure of how to think or feel. I hadn't meant to be so rough with Tisha. I honestly didn't understand why I flipped out on her. A rush of anger took over me and before I knew it, I was treating her like she was my responsibility. The behavior was completely outside of my norm, and once I calmed down, I was extremely embarrassed by it. Owen was asleep by the time I had gotten back to the room, so I crawled into my bed and replayed the scene in my mind at least twenty times before I dozed off.

Martin was teaching Friday's Singles 101 class. Eric had shared quite a bit about the man with me, viewing Martin as a mentor. Although Martin was middle-aged, he had a youthful energy to him, and he came across as a very down-to-earth person. Needing a distraction to keep me from thinking about my blow up on Tisha, I listened intently to Martin's lesson.

"So far we've covered how we should react to difficulties and how to receive from God," Martin started. "Today we will continue on in James chapter one, reviewing verses nine through eleven. Please open your Bibles and I'll start reading at verse nine. It says, 'Let the brother in humble circumstances glory in his elevation—as a Christian, called to the true riches and to be an heir of God. And the rich person ought to glory in being humbled by being shown his human frailty, because like the flower of the grass he will pass away. For the sun comes up with a scorching heat and parches the grass; its flower falls off and its beauty fades away. Even so will the rich man wither and die in the midst of his pursuits.'

"I truly believe that one of the reasons we have to go through hard times in this life is to keep us humble. There is something about struggling that helps a person appreciate what he or she has much more than someone who has been spoiled and given everything without difficulty. Someone who had to work hard and knows what it is like to suffer often perceives people and possessions differently. There is a greater respect and value, not because the person is consumed by the matter, but because he or she knows what it's like to survive without it," Martin said.

"I remember when I got my first car. I had worked hard and saved up the money for it. I was so proud of it and would wash it once a week to keep it looking shiny. Sometimes, I would purposely ride pass people I knew who didn't have a vehicle, just so I could show off. I was only 20-years-old and I had my own set of wheels. I was the man.

"But the car was used and one day the engine went out on it. I only had the car for about a year before the engine died. As you all know, a car is junkyard scrap without a working engine. And most times, engines are so costly that it makes more sense to buy a new car than to fix an engine problem. Well, I didn't have the money to repair the engine or buy a new car. I was so disappointed. I held on to the useless car for a couple months until my father finally made me get rid of it. I sold some of the parts on it and scraped the rest. It took me two more years to save up for another car."

Martin paused and looked out at the crowd before continuing. "The reason I'm telling you all this story is to demonstrate my need for an attitude adjustment. I thought I was 'all that' when I had my car and others couldn't afford one. I forgot what it was like to not have my own form of transportation. I looked down at those who were walking and taking the bus as if they were less than me. But when my car broke down and I had to catch the city bus with them, it forced me to see that I was no better than them. It humbled me to walk again, to have to ask for rides from family and friends. My ego was hurt with the loss of my car, but I had to eventually push past my pride, pick myself up, and start over again.

"Some of you in here today are just like the way I used to be. You think you're special, better than those around you. You're so used to getting everything you want; you're used to life being easy. Maybe you come from a wealthy family, maybe you're naturally attractive and people of the opposite sex have always been drawn to you. Maybe you're the smart one who is successful at everything you touch, or maybe you're charismatic and everyone likes you. Sometimes, when we are blessed and have a little more of a thing than others, we let it go to our heads. Instead of being grateful for the extra and viewing it as a privilege, we see our surplus as a right, exclusive to us and people like us. We throw our excess in others faces as I did when I rode past people walking with a grin on my face. We can be mean, cruel, selfish, and insensitive. But God didn't bless us so that we could act like fools about it. I was supposed to use my car to get to work, church, and wherever else I needed to go, not to show off. But because I used my gift in the wrong way, it was eventually taken from me," Martin said.

"This is one of the points that I want you to get from verses nine through eleven; we should seek to live humble lives. The passage says that the humble person is really the one who should be exalted because his wealth is in God. Alternatively, the rich person, or the one with excess, should only feel glory when he or she is put into situations that remind him of his limitations. What the verse is saying is that by the rich person being made aware of how powerless he or she really is, there is an opportunity for that person to receive true wealth in God.

"Going back to my story about my first car, when I lost my car, I actually found myself. As long as I had that car and was driving around like a king, God could not have the position in my life that He wanted. But when the car broke down, walking humbled me and my experience allowed me to see how I was more like everyone else than I thought. It was then that God could come into my life and use me for His purpose. I had to be brought down in order to be built up. This is the case with many of you. God has to allow you to fall, to go through the fire, to lose everything of importance to you so that He can elevate you. As long as you're on your fake pedestal, you're useless to Him because you are operating in your own strength and with your own limited thinking. You can only do so much by yourself. The Bible says that God's thoughts and ways are higher than ours. He knows the greater things that we cannot even begin to imagine. He wants to take us to the highest mountaintop, but we are satisfied with the tiny hill that we can climb in our own strength. If we want more out of this life, we will have to allow Him to remove our limitations by first taking us into the valley and stripping us of what we value, so that when he elevates us, we will only be concerned with what's of value to Him."

Martin paced back and forth across the platform. "This notion brings up another important point of these verses.

What do you value? Where is your treasure? Where do your riches lie? Are you money hungry? Is everything all about how you can make a quick buck no matter who you hurt or what you have to do to get it? Or is your treasure based on beauty? Are you overly consumed by appearance? Is your own vanity getting in the way of you being the person God created you to be? How many selfies do you have posted on social media? Can people not see God's light in you because all they see is your next picture on Instagram?

"What are your riches? What do you exalt more than God? The humble man realizes that a life with God is more important than any amount of money, beauty, position of power, or anything else considered valuable in this world. As you begin this third day of the conference, consider what you value and if it is keeping you from your divine position in God's kingdom. Think about all of the struggles you've had in your life and how these trials have attempted to humble you and bring you closer to God. Looking back to verse two of the first chapter in James, it tells us to be joyful about our hardships. Now, we are starting to understand why we should be happy that we're going through a hard time. God is allowing the difficulty so that He can bring us into closer relationship with Him. That's why we have you all in Las Vegas. We know some of you are failing miserably at this conference. Some of you can't stay away from the crap tables. Some of you are drinking like fish. Some of you are closing the club down like you work there. We can see the temptation and the struggle in your eyes every morning that you walk into this ballroom. But don't get the wrong impression. We're not trying to set you up for failure, and neither is God. Instead, we want to see you push through the temptation and into your victory. We want to see you all make an intentional decision to choose Christ above all of these worldly options. It won't be easy. Some of you will leave this room in a few minutes and head straight to the slot machines. And if you do, we won't judge you. Just know that when you finally put your value in God, when your riches finally become heaven-focused, nothing that Las Vegas or Atlanta or Los Angeles or New York City or Miami or Chicago or anywhere else in the world that is used to try to trip you up will work because patience will have had its way in your life and you will be complete, lacking nothing. There's beauty at the bottom because most times, that's exactly the place God goes to get His greatest followers."

Lesson 15: Sex and the City

Flee fornication. Every sin that a man doeth is without the body; but he that committeth fornication sinneth against his own body. (I Corinthians 6:18)

Lena

By Friday, I was over trying to party in Vegas. Obviously, it wasn't for me to go out dancing because my only friend at the conference didn't do the nightclub scene and I wasn't willing to follow anyone else's club advice after my traumatic experience at Olympic Gardens. I fully accepted my fate to stay close to the MGM Grand and to entertain myself by gambling instead.

Jessica was really getting into attending the various workshops offered by the conference. Anytime I was around her, she wouldn't shut up about what this or that instructor said. I felt like I had been to each and every session with her as she ran down the who, what, when, where, and why of the lessons. To her benefit, she'd come to Las Vegas to figure out her next move with her long-term boyfriend. I wanted to tell her to just dump the creep. After seven years the man clearly either didn't want marriage at all or didn't want it with her. Nonetheless, I kept my comments to myself. She would have to learn just like everyone else—the hard way.

I was surprised that she didn't spend much time chatting away with her boyfriend on the phone. Most women I knew in relationships couldn't go more than a few hours without talking to, Skyping, or texting the man in their life. For me it was a relief. I certainly didn't want to have to overhear her phone conversations all day and night.

At one point, my curiosity got the best of me and I asked her if it was normal for them to speak so rarely. She said, "Sort of. We don't have that kind of relationship where we are in each other's face every day. We either see each other or speak about every other day. With me being here, I told him that I wouldn't have much time to check-in with him, so he doesn't expect me to call often. I guess I could speak to him more, but I'd rather enjoy myself and focus on the conference. I can always speak to him when I return home."

Not if his other woman takes over while you're gone, I thought. It didn't sound right to me. They'd been together for seven years and didn't speak to each other every day? Plus, he was stalling on the proposal, and he was okay with her going to Las Vegas and not checking in with him daily? I smelled a rat. He must have been using all of his free time with another woman. There was no way that I would be in a serious relationship and allow my man to be so uninvolved. I didn't care much about my friend Douglass, but even we still talked by phone every night.

Speaking of Douglass, the man had finally worked my last nerve. Thursday night after the strip club drama, I called him when I got back to my room because I desperately needed someone to vent to. Douglass was out having a late meal with some friends at a restaurant, so I could barely hear him over all of the background noise, and it seemed he couldn't hear me at all.

"What did you say?" he shouted into the phone.

"I said that I wanted to talk to you. I had a really bad night," I repeated.

"You're going where tonight?"

"No, I said I had a bad night!" I said loudly, beginning to get annoyed.

"Oh, you had a bad night. I'm sorry to hear that, baby. I wish I was there with you."

I sighed, hating how frustrated I felt. "It's not like there's anything you could do. This trip has been a waste of my money."

"What was that?" he asked.

"I said this trip has been a waste of my money!"

"Baby, I can't hear you. I'll call you back when I leave the restaurant so that I can hear you."

"Whatever," I said with an obvious attitude and hung up.

I don't know what I expected, but it angered me that he couldn't talk to me when I really needed him. What good was it to have someone special if he couldn't make you feel special when you needed it most? I sat on my bed fuming. Jessica was still out of the room. It was past the ending time for the karaoke contest that she said she was going to, so I figured she'd met up with some other attendees and was hanging out with them. I noticed that Jessica made friends easily and people seemed to gravitate toward her. Unlike me, Jessica had befriended about ten or so other conference participants, while I, on the other hand, only made a connection with her. She was nice enough to spend most of her time during the day with me, but at night, when I wanted to roam the casino or go out on The Strip, she called her other friends and made plans with them. At least if Jessica would have been in the room with me at that moment, I could have vented to her and felt much better, but instead I felt all alone. I had a few friends back in Atlanta, but there was a three hour time difference between the East Coast and Las Vegas. I was sure that all of my friends were sleeping and would tell me off if I called them.

When thirty minutes passed and neither Jessica had returned to the room nor Douglass had called, I sort of lost it. Grabbing my phone off the nightstand, I redialed Douglass' number. He answered after the third ring.

"Hey, baby. I was just about to call you back. I just got in my car," he said.

"Look, Douglass. This is not working between us. Let's just end it now."

"Lena, what are you talking about?"

"I'm talking about the fact that you weren't there for me when I needed you. I really needed to talk to you tonight, but you were so busy with your friends that you put me off. I expect the man in my life to put me first."

"Lena, you're overreacting. I was at dinner when you called. I was in the middle of eating. I wasn't blowing you off for my friends."

"But I told you that I was having a bad day. You should have gone outside the restaurant for a little while to talk to me."

"Lena, that's crazy. You're expecting too much from me. I would never ask you to stop eating just to talk to me. I would respect the fact that you were having a meal."

"Maybe you're right, Douglass. Maybe I'm expecting too much from you. But someone who wants to be my man has to step up to the plate. It shouldn't be too much to ask a man to be there for me when I'm having a crisis."

"Lena, calm down. I see that I've upset you and I'm sorry for not being available when you were stressed out. I didn't realize that it was that big of an emergency. What happened? Talk to me now."

"No, I don't want to talk to you now. It's too late."

"What's too late, baby?"

"Stop calling me baby! It's too late for us. It's too late for you to listen to me. I'm done. I think you should move on with your life and find someone else. You're not the right man for me, and I'm not the right woman for you."

"Lena, Are you serious?"

"Very."

"And you want me to find someone else?"

"Did I stutter?"

He sighed. "No, no you didn't. Alright then. I guess I'll see you later."

"No you won't. Goodbye, Douglass."

I hung the phone up just as Jessica was walking into the room.

"You okay?" she asked me upon seeing my flustered face.

I shook my head. "Not really, but I will be. I had a horrible night and I just dumped that guy I was seeing back home."

She ran over to my bed. "Oh no! What happened?"

I smiled, glad to see that at least one person cared about me and was willing to listen. Unfortunately, after fussing with Douglass, I was all talked out. "How about we talk about it tomorrow over lunch. Right now, I just want a hot shower and some sleep."

She patted me gentle on the knee and said, "Okay."

Fast forward to Friday, and I felt a little bad about Douglass, but at the same time relieved. I wasn't really into him, so it was probably for the best that I let him go. He was a sweet guy, but I wanted more from a man than just sweet— I wanted passion. Douglass didn't make me feel anything but nauseous.

I agreed to go with Jessica to a workshop Friday afternoon called Sex and the City. From the title, one might assume we'd be watching the movie with Sarah Jessica Parker, but since it was a Christian conference, it was unlikely that would occur.

The instructor was a 30-something-year-old author and psychologist named Dr. Andrea Wilson. From her introduction, we learned that she lived in Rochester, New York, was married to an attractive home builder named Lemuel, and she was four months pregnant with their first child. Her first book, *The Not So Perfect Marriage*, had spent twelve weeks on the New York Times Bestsellers List, peaking at number three. Her second book, *The Cost of Having It All*, was scheduled to release later in the summer and expected to also make the coveted list.

"This session, Sex and the City, is not about Kerry Bradshaw or her other nymphomaniac friends. Instead, we will explore society's perception of premarital sex, especially in urban environments," Dr. Wilson said.

"So, let's begin with a basic question. How does our society view sex among unmarried people?" she asked.

At first, no one responded, but after several silent seconds, Jessica answered, "That it's okay to have sex if you're not married."

Dr. Wilson nodded. "Okay. Anyone else?"

A man in the front row spoke up and said, "That single people should be free to have sex with whomever they choose."

A girl in the back raised her hand and said, "Sex is what you do if you like someone, even if you don't plan to marry them."

Another woman near the back said, "If you're not having sex, something is wrong with you."

A guy in the fifth row said, "Everyone is having sex and it is necessary if you want to be in a relationship."

"Excellent answers," Dr. Wilson said. "So as single people, based on those answers, how does that make you all feel?"

Once again, Jessica answered first. "Like a man isn't going to be faithful or marry me if I don't put out."

"It makes me feel guilty for wanting to wait," one woman said.

"Like I shouldn't try to control my sexual urges," a man said.

"As if sex is no longer reserved for marriage. No one is going to respect you if you hold out," another woman said.

"As a man, if I'm not having sex, it's like I feel like less than a man," another guy said.

"I appreciate the honesty I am hearing in this room," Dr. Wilson said. "This isn't an easy topic, but the fact that you all came to this workshop today and are willing to talk about it says that you want to do things God's way and not the world's way. And I'm going to tell you this, God honors those who are obedient to him. The enemy wants you to think that if you don't have sex, no one is going to love or accept you, but that is a lie. God will honor your decision to remain virtuous and bring the right person who can reap the benefits of your waiting if you trust Him.

"In today's session, I want to start by dispelling five big myths about being single and having sex. I just told you the first. Myth number one, no one will love or want a virgin or celibate person. Myth number two, you won't enjoy sex after marriage if you don't test drive the car in advance. Myth number three, you can't control your sexual urges. Myth number four, God doesn't want you to have any fun. And myth number five, plenty of people have sex before marriage and it does not hurt their marriages. I want to also cover a few other topics, so I'll jump right in with the myths for the sake of time.

"No one will love or want you if you're not having sex. That's a lie. Which reminds me, every time I say 'that's a lie,' you have to say 'from the pit.' Of course, we're referring to the pit of Hell. When it comes to the enemy's lies, we have to call them out for what they are. So let's try it now. That's a lie . . ." Dr. Wilson said.

"From the pit," the crowd said back.

"Uh unn. That was horrible. That was the weakest confrontation I've ever heard. You know how someone says something crazy to you or about you, and you go find the person and call them out? You have to say it with passion like you really mean it. Let's try it again," Dr. Wilson said. "That's a lie . . ."

"From the pit!" we yelled back.

"No one will want to marry you because you're not having sex. That's a lie . . ."

"From the pit!"

"You can't have a satisfying sex like when you're married if you haven't tested the equipment first. That's a lie . . ."

"From the pit!"

"Why even try? You cannot control your sexual urges. That's a lie . . ."

"From the pit!"

"You know why single Christians can't have sex? God doesn't want you to have any fun. That's a lie . . ."

"From the pit!"

"Having sex before marriage cannot hurt your marriage in any way. That's a lie . . ."

"From the pit!"

"That's what I'm talking about! You all got it," Dr. Wilson said. "This is how you have to deal with a liar. You have to call a liar out, because it you don't, they'll keep on lying to you. They will think they got away with the first lie, so they'll create more and more lies until everything they say to you is a lie. I don't know about you all, but I don't have time for a bunch of lies in my life. I'm trying to live my life to the fullest. So the next time the enemy comes at me with a lie, something that I know is in the Bible, a word God gave to me so that I could live the best life possible, I'm going to get all in his face and say, 'That's a lie. . .'"

"From the pit!" we all yelled out again.

"Now, I told you all that I was going to dispel these myths, right?"

"Yeah," the group said.

"Let me do that right now. I'm going to change your life with this one. Are you all listening?" she asked.

"Yeah."

"I only need one verse from the Bible to dispel all five of those myths. You all ready for it?"

"Yeah."

"Here it is. Numbers chapter 23, verse 19. I'm going to give it to you in two versions. First the King James Version says, 'God is not a man, that he should lie; neither the son of man, that he should repent: hath he said, and shall he not do it? Or hath he spoken, and shall he not make it good?' A different version of the Bible called The Message, reads, 'God is not man, one given to lies, and not a son of man changing his mind. Does he speak and not do what he says? Does he promise and not come through?'"

Dr. Wilson shook her head with excitement. "The reason we can call these myths out because anything and everything God says is true. He's not a liar. The devil is a liar. Your new boyfriend or girlfriend might be a liar. Your friends may be liars, but God is not a man and He does not lie. If He said in his Word that you can do all things through Him who gives you strength, you can control your sexual urges. If He says that He can supply all of your needs, He can give you the love you need and make sure you get it exactly the way you need it. You don't have to test drive God's choice. Imagine if you really needed a car, and someone came to you one day and said, 'I know you need a car. I have a lot of cars that I own, so I thought about what you like and I picked out one of my cars especially for you. I'm giving it to you, free of charge. Here's the keys, it's yours.' Are you really going to tell the person, 'Wait? Hold up. Before I accept your car, let me test drive it. And if I don't like the way it rides, I don't want it.' No, you're going to thank the person, click your heels in the air, and take your new car down to the tag and title office to put it in your name. You won't care how that car drives, as long as it does. Am I right?"

"Right," the crowd said and laughed.

"But God isn't going to give you a bootleg car. It might not be perfect, but that's because he wants to see you spruce it up and make it your own. In the same manner, God will give you a mate specially designed for you. That person might not seem perfect at first, but if you clean him or her up, and for the fellas, put your last name on her, show your mate some love, after a while, you'll step back and see that person is perfect for you. God doesn't pass out lemons," Dr. Wilson said.

"Don't let the devil fool you. God has great plans for you. Don't let the enemy lie to you. You can live a Christian life. You can receive all that God has for you. You don't have to compromise yourself for a chance at love. You can be virtuous and in right standing with God. He's not a liar. If He said it, it will come to pass. He has no reason to lie to you. What will

God gain from lying? He doesn't have to lie because He holds all power in His hands. He doesn't have to trick you. He's not withholding fun from you. God made fun. The first fun thing in this world, God made. He made jokes, He made smiles, He made laughter, He made humor, He made sex, and made sex pleasurable. He doesn't have to keep you from any of the good things in life because when He made it all He said, 'It is good,' and gave man and woman dominion over it. The devil is a liar. Call him out. When he comes at you with all of that negative, unproductive, un-Christ-like jibber jabber, just tell him, that's a lie . . .'"

"From the pit!" I yelled. *Perfect for me? Had I been too hasty about Douglass?*

Lesson 16: Don't Let Your Imagination Get the Best of You

For the weapons of our warfare are not carnal, but mighty through God to the pulling down of strong holds. Casting down imaginations, and every high thing that exalteth itself against the knowledge of God, and bringing into captivity every thought to the obedience of Christ.
(II Corinthians 10:4-5)

Tisha

Nelson's behavior Thursday night had really thrown me for a loop. After thinking about the situation, I understood his point—I should have told my friends where I was going—but he didn't have to come to me so forceful about it. I hadn't planned on leaving the club with Larry, but one minute we were dancing, and the next, he was asking me if I wanted to sit down and talk. I was assuming that he meant somewhere in the club, but when he led me out of the door, I was stumped.

"Where are we going?" I asked as I continued to walk next to him pass the Rainforest Café.

"There's a Starbucks over there," he pointed out. "I thought it would be a quieter place to talk so that we won't have to yell at each other over the music," he explained.

"Oh. Good idea."

We went into Starbucks and ordered a couple of lattes. Sitting down in a pair of cozy chairs, we talked about our individual lives and what brought us to Vegas. Larry lived in Los Angeles and frequently drove out to Las Vegas to golf, gamble, and relax. He and another doctor owned a private practice where they mostly did breast augmentations (implants) and rhinoplasty (nose jobs), but could be hired to alter almost any part of the human body. When I asked him why he chose plastic surgery as a profession out of all of the specialties in medicine, he simply said, "For the money. Why else?"

I thought about his answer the next night as I prepared to go out on a date with him. As much as I cherished a man with money, I also wanted a man whose ambition was more than merely wealth. I made decent money because in addition to being a principal, I also taught college education courses online. I had bills to pay, and working in education at the secondary level was known to be a low paying gig. However, I loved my job; it was the passion for it that kept me there when the paychecks and the stress weren't enough. I was hoping to move upward into senior administration because the promotion would give me a much higher salary while still being able to work in the field that I enjoyed. If I was going to ever be in a serious relationship, I wanted to be with someone who could relate to feeling a sense of purpose in their work. Making money was great, but wasn't there more to success?

Have I completely lost my mind?

I couldn't believe that I was thinking thoughts like that. The Tisha everyone knew was all about a man who could provide for me and treat me like a queen, a very expensive queen. Although I toyed with good looking men making minimum wage, I only dated six figure men with an escrow account and an American Express Centurion Card, better known as a Black Card. But ever since I'd come to Las Vegas, I'd been entertaining dating down and not being so concerned with wealth. I guess it had a lot to do with my intentions.

Previous to the trip, I never planned to settle down with any of the men I spent time with, so for me it was like they had to pay me for my time. But now, I was starting to wonder if I wanted or needed more from a man than just a shopping spree or a pricey dinner. This religious conference was starting to get to me, to change me, yet I wasn't exactly sure if it was for the better or for the worse.

As I finished getting dressed for dinner with Larry, I replayed my altercation with Nelson again in my mind. The intensity in his eyes was straight murderous. If looks were daggers, both Larry and I would be in body bags by now. When Larry tried to get involved, I became nervous. I appreciated the sentiment, but I could handle Nelson on my own. The last thing I wanted was a brawl in Starbuck between Nelson and Larry on my account. So when Nelson grabbed me by my wrist, I didn't pull away until we were in the hallway. I tried to save face and let Nelson know that I didn't like him butting in my business, but he hit me with a line that I didn't expect.

"Maybe that's the problem. Maybe I'm the only one who really cares," he'd said.

After he walked away, I stood there for several seconds with my mouth agape, trying to process what just happened. None of it made sense, so I pushed my confused thoughts aside and returned to Larry inside the coffee shop. I thought I could continue our conversation from where we'd left off, but I couldn't seem to focus. I had way too many questions in my head and not enough answers. Feigning fatigue, I ended my time with Larry. He allowed me to walk away from him only after I promised to have dinner with him on Friday. Less than 24 hours later, I sprayed myself with one of my favorite perfumes before I took one last glance in the mirror and headed down the elevator to meet Larry at FiAMMA, an Italian restaurant in The District section of MGM Grand.

I met Larry at the restaurant and we were promptly seated. We had a delightful conversation over Maine Lobster Gnocchi and Raviolini, which is FiAMMA's specialty short rib ravioli.

After dinner, Larry invited me to go outside for a walk up The Strip with him.

It was a warm night, the sky was clear, and the lights of Vegas made The Strip appear to sparkle. I could never get enough of the Las Vegas skyline, and I would miss it dearly once I went home. I took several pictures with my camera phone of the city, me, and Larry and me together. Hanging with him was nice, but I couldn't seem to get Nelson and the rest of my mini crew out of my mind. I wondered if they were having a good time at the club without me. Did they miss me? Did they even notice that I wasn't there? I imagined Owen hugging the wall and turning pretty girls away left and right. He was really committed to his fiancée back home, and we all had to respect him for that.

I pictured Sky trying to out dance some barely legal girl and passing her phone number to a guy ten or more years her junior. Despite all of Sky's flirting, she hadn't really given any of the men who took her bait the time of day. I had come to realize that it was all for fun and Sky just wanted to see if she still could be young at heart.

I visualized Nelson passing Sky drinks from the bar that some silly woman had purchased for him. The ladies really did seem to latch onto Nelson, but he always maintained a nonchalant attitude and took it all in stride . . . except when it came to me.

"Did you hear what I just said?" Larry asked, pulling me out of my daze.

"Huh? Sorry. I must have zoned out, thinking about the conference and all. Please repeat what you said."

"I asked you if you wanted to come up to my room and maybe talk for a while longer," he said smoothly.

I gave him an incredulous look. Did he think that because he bought me dinner that I was going to sleep with him?

"Your hotel room?" I asked him. In my mind I was begging for him to change his question.

"Yeah, at the Mirage. It's only a few blocks away. I have this spectacular view that I know you're going to love."

I bet. This was another reason I was starting to change my thoughts about casual dating. So many men, especially in Atlanta, assumed that just because I smiled at them and gave them my digits, they would get to know me in the Biblical sense. I wasn't easy, and I wasn't interested in a one night stand. Larry had me confused with one of these low-self-esteem women crawling around Las Vegas and lined up in his practice's waiting room.

"No, I don't think that's a good idea," I said, trying to let him down nicely. I was a bit insulted by the offer, but he was a man. It was likely to happen at some point.

"Why not? We just had a lovely meal, and I would really like to get to know you better. I think we could have something special," he said, laying the charm on thick.

I wanted to roll my eyes, but that would have been too obvious. I didn't want him to think that I used him for a free dinner, but my love was going to cost a whole lot more than an Italian dinner and coffee at Starbucks.

"I have more classes in the morning, so I think I need to get back to my own room. Thanks for a fantastic evening," I said, giving him a friendly peck on the cheek. That was the closest he would ever get to *knowing* me. I wasn't for sale or rent.

"Awe, come on, Tisha. Just for a little while," he pleaded.

"Not tonight," I said before waving goodbye to him and heading back down Las Vegas Boulevard—alone.

Lesson 17: Life or Death?
The Choice is Yours

Then when lust hath conceived, it bringeth forth sin: and sin, when it is finished, bringeth forth death. (James 1:15)

Nelson

Friday night, we ventured out to Marquee nightclub at the Cosmopolitan—without Tisha. I'll admit, it felt awkward to leave her behind, but she insisted that we go without her. I knew the reasons why she passed up on the chance to hang out with us—she was probably still mad at me and she wanted to see the mystery man who kept popping up like a stalker. Hey, if that was the kind of man she was into, who was I to stop her? She had made it painfully clear the night prior that she and I were just friends and that she'd rather spend her time with stalker boy.

The Marquee, like the other clubs we'd been to in Vegas, was filled to the brim with people who partied like their lives depended on it. Out of the few spots we'd checked out, Marquee was my favorite. They seemed to cater more to a mixed crowd than the others. There was actually a Boom Box Room they played Hip Hop the entire night while the main area blasted House music. Ready for variety, Owen, Sky, and I spent our time at the Marquee in the Boom Box Room, needing respite from all of the House and Techno we'd heard over the past few days. When the song "Shots" by came on, I jumped up out of my seat, ordered a round of lemon drop shots for our crew, and found myself wishing Tisha was with us to enjoy the moment.

On Saturday, I sat in the Singles 101 class, looking around, hoping I would spot Tisha. She hadn't been in her room when we'd dropped Sky off after leaving the Marquee—it figured. I just wanted to see her face to know that she was alright. I knew I was acting soft when it came to her, yet I couldn't help but want to protect her. Despite my womanizing ways, at my core I was a Hayes, and Hayes men always looked out for the women in their lives.

Was Tisha the woman in my life?

No.

The class was about to begin when I noticed Tisha and Sky slide inside the room and find two seats near the rear. My heart raced then relaxed as I felt a twinge of excitement then peace at seeing her and knowing she'd made it back to her room in one piece.

Lydia was teaching the day's Singles 101 class and immediately jumped into the scripture reading. "Blessed, happy, to be envied is the man who is patient under trial and stands up under temptation, for when he has stood the test and been approved, he will receive the victor's crown of life which God has promised to those who love Him. Let no one say when he is tempted, I am tempted from God; for God is incapable of being tempted by what is evil and He Himself tempts no one. But every person is tempted when he is drawn away, enticed and baited by his own evil desires, lust, passions. Then the evil desire, when it has conceived, gives birth to sin, and sin, when it is fully matured, brings forth death. Do not be misled, my beloved brethren."

Lydia scanned the crowd. "Today we are studying James chapter one, verses 12 through 16. I know that you all have been given a lot of information since the start of the conference. Not only do you have these morning Singles classes with Martin and I, you also are attending breakout sessions throughout the day. Based on what I am hearing, you all have received a lot of inspiring messages during the various workshops. I hope you are all taking good notes so that you can utilize this insight when you return home tomorrow afternoon.

"So to recap, on Wednesday I spoke about having joy despite your trials. On Thursday, Martin discussed being single-minded, and on Friday, he let you know that God can work with a humble spirit. Today, I want to speak with you all about life and death. When Christians mention life and death, we could be referring to earthly life and death or spiritual life and death. We all understand that we as humans live a life on this earth and that at some point, we will experience death. We are mortal beings and we will eventually die. However, there is the life and death of our spirit man, and this variation of the terms are connected to our eternal destinations. As Christians, we believe that through Christ, we can have eternal life and never have to face eternal death, often referred to as eternal damnation.

"Don't worry, this is not a fire and brimstone lesson, but I point these terms out because we all have a choice. God has given us free will to choose how we will experience both this world and the world beyond. We can either make a conscious choice, or the choice will be made for us by default. James chapter one, verses 12 through16 reminds us of the two choices laid before us, life and death, victory or defeat.

"When you all came to this conference, we told you on the first day that you had a choice to make. You could come to the sessions and take in as much inspirational materials and resources as your heart desired, or you could go out into the hotel and the streets of Las Vegas and receive what the world offers. The choice has been yours this entire time. We've never forced you to participate with us, with exception to the daily Singles 101 classes. Everything else has been up to you to make the decision," Lydia said.

"And now that we're down to our last two classes, I will tell you why we made the Singles 101 classes mandatory. The biggest reason we did it was to ensure your safety. With over 200 attendees, it would be nearly impossible to keep up with everyone and be sure that you all were safe during the entire conference. By making this meeting mandatory, we have been able to keep an accurate head count from day to day.

"The other reason we made attendance to these classes a requirement was because we wanted to make sure that each day your choice between life and death was presented to you. As we just read, sin leads to death while overcoming sin leads to life eternal. Every day, and all through the night, Las Vegas presents the choice of sin and death to its visitors. In the midst of the allure of The Strip and the temptations that surround it, we needed to offer you another option. We needed to offer you a chance to pick God and His way. Now, let me be clear. Just because you had fun on the Las Vegas Strip doesn't mean that you chose death or sin. Vegas is an exciting place full of enjoyable activities for the entire family, and not all of the amenities are bad. But lurking behind every door in Sin City is sin itself, and its desire is to consume you, to lead you down the path of death. Verse sixteen warns us not to be deceived or misled. This must be stated because sin is very tricky. For example, you might think, I'm going to just put five dollars in this slot machine. Gambling is not really all that bad. I'm not hurting anyone and it's only five dollars. Right?

"But when five dollars runs out and you've warmed up that machine, you rationalize that five dollars more is still not a big deal. The next thing you know, you're hundreds or even thousands of dollars in the hole. You might have spent your rent money or entire paycheck. You might have borrowed money from your credit card or worse, a loan shark. Now you're up to your head in debt and people are looking for you or taking your possessions because you just wanted to put five dollars into the slot machine."

Lydia sighed. "I'm not judging any of you who have gambled, or partied, or consumed alcohol, or anything else while you've been here. You have had a choice to do all of these things and you've made your choices along the way, right or wrong. You still have one more day, and you still get to choose today which path you will take. Don't make any decisions to please me or for my benefit. The choice you make will only matter if it comes from your heart, from your desire to either please yourself or please God. Today, right now, I'm just offering you another chance. Martin and I, as well as the rest of the conference staff, are standing in the gap for you all, and in love, we extend the path that leads back to God and to everlasting life. Which will you choose? You can suffer through the hardest trials of your life, endure the biggest temptations in this world and still choose life. It's all up to you."

Lesson 18: Your Reputation Precedes You

Furthermore, he must have a good reputation among outsiders, so that he does not fall into disgrace and the Devil's trap.
(I Timothy 3:7, Holman Christian Standard Bible)

Tisha

Amber practically begged me to attend a workshop on Saturday called Salvaging Your Reputation. When I asked her why, she said, "Just wait. You'll see."

When we walked into the meeting room where the session was schedule, I almost fell out. Johnathan Gold, Amber's ex-fiancé, was the session's instructor. He stood behind the podium, greeting people as they came in with a head nod and a wave. When he saw us, he tilted his head in acknowledgement and smiled. I held back a scream as we took our seats several rows away from the front.

"What is he doing here? Did you know about this?" I asked Amber the moment we sat down.

"He's teaching the workshop and yes, I knew about it. I was the one who recommended him."

I shoved her in the side with my elbow. "You've got to be kidding me. Does Eric know about this?"

"Eric knows. The only reason he's not here with us is because one of the presenters got sick and had to cancel. Eric is covering the guy's class in another room," Amber said.

"This is so unbelievable. You could have at least warned me. This is the second time that you didn't divulged need to know information to me. The first was when you invited Nelson to the conference and put us next to each other on the airplane."

"Like that was such a bad thing," Amber said. "You and Nelson are like best friends now. I can barely get a moment alone with you without Nelson tagging along."

"I know you aren't talking, Mrs. Eric Hayes. I'm surprised we've seen each other at all during this conference. If you aren't working, you're all hugged up with your hubby," I shot back.

"Touché. I'm sorry I didn't tell you about Gold . . . or about Nelson. You don't have to stay here in the session if you don't want. I'm just interested in what he's going to disclose in his presentation. I'm dying to hear what he has to say about that Green Global disaster," she said, referring to a business partnership that she'd almost entered into with Gold, which ended up going sour.

My curiosity was instantly peaked. "Ooh. He's going to talk about that? In that case, I'm staying!"

Amber glanced at me and smiled. Neither of us could tear ourselves away from a bit of old fashion nosiness.

Gold started his presentation a few minutes later. "Good afternoon, everyone. My name is Johnathan Gold and I'll be spending several minutes with you all today on the topic of your reputation. I am the founding partner of an international investment company based out of Atlanta, Georgia. I wish I could say that I've always maintained a good reputation, but that's far from the truth. I've hurt people along the way, burned bridges, and put myself in a few bad situations. I'm not sure how many of you are professionals or business owners, but if you are, please know that your reputation precedes you. People will make decisions about their willingness to work with and for you based on the word circling your industry about you. I had to learn this lesson the hard way, so it is my intention to help spare you all unnecessary anguish with this session.

"Even if you are not a business owner or have a certain profession, maintaining a good reputation is still essential. Everyone plays a role in society, and each one of you have something that you do and someone you are important to. For example, you might volunteer at your church or you might have children. In both cases, you want others to have a positive perception of you, for the most part, so that you can continue to positively impact your church or your children."

Gold cleared his throat and continued. "There are two important aspects of this topic that I want to explore: protection and salvaging. Protecting your reputation is a lot like preventative health care; you implement healthy strategies in advance to avoid getting sick. The same goes for your reputation. There are ways that you can incorporate wise behaviors into your life and career in an attempt to keep your reputation out of harm's way. One strategy is heeding to good advice. The Bible tell us to use wise counsel. Sometimes God will place people in your life that can warn you or direct you in your path. Now, you have to be careful because every person who offers advice isn't qualified to give it to you. Some people don't know what they are talking about, and others have hidden agendas concerning your path. But if you have someone in your life who you are certain has the knowledge to help you and is trustworthy, you really want to take the time to consider his or her suggestions. A colleague of mine, Amber Ross-Hayes, is here today. Some years back we were going into a business deal and she found out some pretty negative information about the venture we were investing into. She attempted to warn me and my partner about the issue, but we were so determined to make the deal work that we ignored her. Well, she was right, and my company paid a hefty price to both our finances and our reputation for our mistake."

Gold glanced at Amber who nudged me. She'd probably been waiting on that public apology for years.

"Another example of protection when it comes to your reputation is keeping your word. A lot of businesses get into trouble for the mere fact that they don't follow through. If I establish a business relationship with you and I don't keep my end of the agreement, not only will you refuse to deal with me in the future, but you're likely to tell everyone who will listen about how poorly I dealt with you. Now, you all might not be business owners, but this same idea work with friendships, family members, your education, and any other area of life. If your boyfriend says he's going to take you out to dinner, you are going to expect it. If he doesn't take you out, his lack of follow through is going to negatively impact your ability to trust him. Sooner or later, if he continues to let you down, you're either going to break up with him or have a dysfunctional relationship because the trust has dissolved over time. His reputation with you is ruined," Gold said.

"So far, some of you may be listening to me speak, thinking what I am saying has absolutely nothing to do with you. Your reputation is fine, and you already understand the importance of having a positive image at work or in your community. Am I right?" he asked.

No one verbally responded, but there were several head nods and all eyes remained focused on him, anticipating what he would say next.

"The reason that I was asked to speak on this topic is because in today's society it is evident that people are forgetting the value of a good reputation. We may know that a good reputation is important, but our actions, especially in relation to social media, are devastating to our personal and professional outlook. Because of technology, information about all of us is not only easy to access, but easy to spread. One bad word about you can 'go viral' in a matter of minutes. As a businessman, before working with a new client or associate, and especially before hiring someone, I Google them. I want to know where their reputation stands. I cannot afford to have my company negatively impacted by someone else's poor image. I've worked too hard to clean up my own bad rep, so I cannot allow another's mistakes to undo all of what I've built and rebuilt. This class is for you because each of you have a reputation to build and to protect. If you fail to maintain a positive image of yourself, future opportunities may be denied to you because of your bad reputation."

Gold paused and scanned the crowd. "What does this mean for you? It means that you must be careful about the things that you say and do in public, which includes social media. If you have a potty mouth, censor yourself because employers are checking out your Facebook page and Twitter accounts. Avoid posting those pictures online of you and your friends partying like there's no tomorrow. Stop arguing with people online and revealing in-depth details about your personal life and relationships. Others are watching what you do and say, and your reputation is at risk. And I will take it a bit further and mention that if you are a Christian, a lot of this stuff not only negatively impacts your reputation, it also dims your light in this world. How are you supposed to answer the calling to go out into the world and spread the gospel if no one values you because of your tarnished image?"

The room was so quiet you could hear a pin drop. I was all about keeping a glowing reputation for the sake of my career and personal life, but I hadn't considered the ramifications that my image had on my religious beliefs. Honestly, until this conference, I hadn't put much effort at all into considering God. I figured that as long as I stayed out of trouble, lived a decent life, and said a prayer from time to time, I was good. Yet maybe God wanted more from me than just for me to live decently, and possibly, my whole job drama was His way of getting my attention. It certainly had led me to this singles conference. I couldn't deny that the daily lessons were doing a number on my heart and mind. I hadn't expected this event to have such an influence on me, and even though the messages were probably for my good, I couldn't help but internally fight against embracing them as new truths in my life.

"That brings me to my next point," Gold continued. "Alternatively, you need to also be prepared to salvage your reputation. Sometimes, even if you are doing all of the right things, either a lie will be formed about you or someone will become displeased with you and use their displeasure against you to hurt your reputation. For example, a competitor in business may not like the fact that you're outselling them. So they may tell someone else in the industry that your work is subpar or that you're not a nice person. Little negative words may be spoken about you behind closed doors even though you haven't done anything wrong. It is in these cases that salvaging your reputation is vital. Even if you have messed up, like I've done in my past, there are still ways to control the damage and restore your reputation.

"One of the best things you can do to salvage your reputation is to be honest. The more you lie or attempt to cover up a matter, usually the worse it becomes. If you find yourself in a sticky situation, take courage and be honest," Gold said.

"Another important step in salvaging your reputation is rebuilding trust. When your reputation gets mired, trust is broken. Until you rebuild trust, you will find yourself caught in this damaging position. With the example of the boyfriend who doesn't follow through, if he was to admit he was wrong—being honest—and then try to rebuild trust by actually following through on a few commitments he's made to you, you would be likely to give him another chance. But until he demonstrates a change in behavior through rebuilding trust, you're always going to perceive him in a pessimistic light.

"Finally, you want to seek outside help. You can't always fix every problem on your own. Often, you need an ally to assist you in restoring your name. As Christians, our number one ally is God. The bible says that vengeance is God's. We don't have to try to get back at someone who tried to hurt our reputation. God will handle that person without you making a bigger mess of the situation. You have to use your help. Look to God to help rebuild your name. In the process, He will bring other allies into your corner who also have the ability to stand beside you as you recover from the crisis.

"We are all sinners and have fallen short of God's glory. We have all made mistakes in our personal and professional lives that have negatively influenced how people view us. Thank God that He does not hold our sins against us, but people do. Therefore you must be both proactive and reactive in regards to your public image. God has great plans for you and a poor reputation can keep you from your dreams if you allow it," Gold said.

I had to blink to make sure that I wasn't imagining the scene. Johnathan Gold was in Las Vegas at a Christian singles conference, teaching a session about having a good reputation. And what was even more unbelievable was that his session was so enlightening, it actually had me reflecting on my own life. I had seen—and heard—it all. Amber sat next to me, listening intently and beaming with pride. Her relationship with Gold undoubtedly had a positive influence on him. Johnathan Gold was a completely different man from the person Amber dated six years ago. If an egotistical man like Gold could change, I had faith that someone like Nelson could change too. And maybe even me.

Lesson 19: Hidden Agendas Always Come to Light

Therefore whatsoever ye have spoken in darkness shall be heard in the light; and that which ye have spoken in the ear in closets shall be proclaimed upon the housetops.
(Luke 12:3)

Lena

My trip to Vegas was winding down, and so far it had been nothing like I had expected. When I initially registered for the conference, I imagined myself being the life of the party, winning jackpots, and showing Eric just what he missed out on when he chose Amber over me. But up to this point, I had accomplished none of these goals. Truthfully, I was being counterproductive. I had lost over $300 playing slot machines and Bingo, the only club I had been to was a strip club—that was by mistake—and Eric was avoiding me like the plague.

I was feeling as if I needed to do something drastic to get his attention, so I dug deeper into Jonelle's birthday party money and made dinner reservations for Eric and me at Joël Robuchon, an award-winning restaurant at the MGM Grand, specializing in French cuisine. I pretended to be Lydia Woods, and paid the concierge to call Eric's room and request only his presence at dinner to discuss a male mentoring program. I figured Eric and Amber would believe my lie if the Woods were involved and it had to do with helping others. That night, the conference was having a Stag Ball at 8:00 p.m. in which everyone dressed up and purposely went dateless. Having an early dinner with Eric would work out perfectly considering the wait staff would only be serving appetizers at the ball. As anticipated, Eric accepted the invitation and I prepared myself for a pivotal evening with my ex.

I dressed in a sexy red cocktail dress and matching red heels. After pinning my hair in a classy up-do, I applied enough makeup to accent my already attractive facial features, but not too much to avoid appearing desperate. Dinner was scheduled for 6:00 p.m., so I purposely arrived at 6:10 to make the surprise effective. I didn't want to get there early or on-time and risk him seeing me and running away. I figured by the time I'd arrived, they would have already seated him and he would be forced to sit through the meal with me. Sure enough, when I walked into the restaurant and provided the name of my party—Hayes—they informed me that my guest had been seated already.

Taking a deep breath in, I allowed the hostess to usher me to my table. The restaurant was elegantly decorated with royal purple velvet walls and chairs. Gold and black chandeliers hung from the ceiling and each table was accented with golden stick candles. The lighting was low, creating a romantic ambiance, and I immediately knew I had selected the perfect atmosphere for our time together. It would be well worth the unplanned expenses . . . so I thought.

As the hostess stopped in front of my table, I made eye contact with my guest, and my mouth flew open, letting out a loud gasp.

"Is there something wrong?" the hostess asked me, noticing my shocked expression.

"Everything's fine," my guest answered for me. "Lena, please have a seat. I'm sure you can't wait to order something off this delightful menu."

I nodded weakly and sat down in the chair that the hostess had pulled out for me. She laid a white cloth napkin over my lap and handed me a menu before walking away.

I looked up at my guest, ignoring the menu in my hand. "What are *you* doing here?" I asked in a hush voice, but with iciness in my tone.

Amber smiled brightly as if she was extremely proud of herself. "I could ask you the same thing, but I think we both already know the answer to that."

I looked away from her. My attention went to a far wall that was designed to imitate floor to ceiling manicured bushes. Though minutes ago I was enchanted by the décor of the restaurant, now it felt silly and overdone.

"What do you want?" I asked her, refusing to make eye contact with her again.

"The question is not what *I* want, but what *you* want. Why would you go through the trouble of pretending to be Lydia and inviting my husband out to dinner with you? What are you up to?"

"Nothing," I said. "I just wanted to have a nice dinner with the father of my child. Is that a crime?"

The waiter approached our table ready to take our drink orders.

"I'll have a glass of white wine," I said, feeling like I needed something with a kick to help me cope with my uncomfortable scenario.

"Water with lemon," Amber said. The waiter nodded and walked away.

I glanced at Amber who was twirling her diamond and platinum wedding ring around her finger. I wondered if she was purposely trying to annoy me.

"No, it's not a crime to have dinner with the father of your child," Amber said, continuing our conversation. "But it is a problem when you're dishonest about it. You attempted to lure Eric here under false pretenses. You're wearing a skin tight dress and hooker shoes. Obviously, you meant to both ambush Eric and turn him on at the same time. So, being his wife and all, I'm obligated to question your intentions. As I sat here for ten minutes waiting on your arrival, I came up with only two reasonable explanations."

I really hated this woman. She was so smug that I wanted to grab one of the lit candles and set her hair on fire. She wouldn't think she was so smart then. "Let's hear these so-called reasonable explanations," I said.

"Why don't we just skip my guesses and you can just tell me the truth."

I laughed in her face. "Amber, as exciting as it may be for you, I'm getting bored of playing this impromptu game of Clue. What do you want me to say? I killed Eric in the dining room with the lead pipe?"

"Okay," she said, leaning in closer as if to tell me a secret. "Since you want to be difficult, I'll just go ahead and tell you my thoughts. I think that you came all the way to Vegas believing that you could somehow win Eric's heart back during the trip. I think that you don't really love him, you just hate seeing him with me. I think you attempted to lure him to dinner tonight to either seduce him or to trick me into thinking something is going on between the two of you. I also think that you are too old to be playing these childish games and that you need to grow up. Eric is married to me. If you would finally get that through your thick skull maybe you could let him go long enough to allow a decent man to get to know you, love you, and marry you."

I shook my head slowly to let her know that her confrontation didn't scare me. "You think you know me, but you have no idea what you're talking about."

She twisted her lips. I could see that I was frustrating her. She shouldn't have come to the table if she wasn't prepared to play my way.

"Oh really? Well let me tell you this," she said, tapping her index fingernail hard against the table. "I might not *know* what I'm talking about, but I sure figured out your little charade tonight. I also *know* that if I ever see you trying to push up on my husband again, your clothing will be red, but not because that's the color of the fabric."

I couldn't believe she threatened me. *The devil is busy,* I thought.

"That's really Christian of you, Amber. What happened to turning the other cheek? Isn't that what Jesus said?" I asked.

She sucked her teeth. "Oh, I'll turn the other cheek alright—your cheek to knock you upside you head from both angles. Don't worry about my Christianity. I'll repent afterward."

If I couldn't have dinner with Eric because of Amber, at least I could rile her up. "I thought you were supposed to be here in a leadership position, to help mentor us lowly single people," I said, feigning maturity.

Amber rolled her eyes. "Lena, save it. You've been at this conference almost five days and you haven't heard a thing we've all been trying to tell you. Why did you come if you weren't interested in growing?"

"According to you, I came to seduce your husband."

Amber threw her napkin on the table. "This is pointless, I'm leaving."

Relief coursed through my veins. "Good."

She offered me a mischievous smile. "Oh yeah. I hope you don't mind, but since I got here before you did, I took it upon myself to order dinner to go for me and Eric. It's not often that someone takes us out to such an exclusive restaurant. Thanks for the meal, Lena. Make sure you leave the waiter an 18 percent tip."

She stood up and headed for the exit. I wanted to scream when I watched the waiter hand her two large take out bags. She had pulled a fast one on me; I didn't even think she had it in her. Who would have guessed that Amber would have out-schemed me? Now I was left picking up the tab for her and Eric's dinner.

The traitorous waiter returned to the table a few seconds later and asked, "Are you ready to order?"

"No," I said, feeling defeated. "You can just bring me the bill."

I almost choked when I received the bill—$250 . . . and it didn't include the tip.

Tisha

Although we were all partied out, my Vegas crew agreed to visit one last club on our final night in town. Everyone we spoke to raved about a spot called XS Nightclub inside the Wynn hotel, so it was only necessary that we experienced XS for ourselves before heading back to our separate homes and cities. Our agreement was to attend the Stag Ball from 8:00 p.m. until 9:00 p.m. and then to head over to the Wynn hotel before the line for the club became too long.

I wore a yellow halter top dress with peek-a-boo shoes. Sky had on a sky blue sheer top with a white camisole underneath and white bootcut dress pants. Our attire was dressy, but not overly done considering we were going straight from the ball to the club. When we got to the Stag Ball, we spotted Nelson and Owen shoveling pot stickers into their mouths. It was insane because we had all just had dinner less than an hour and a half prior at Shibuya, a Japanese steakhouse at the MGM. It was a little lazy on our part that as a group, we hadn't ventured outside of the MGM Grand for dinner on any night during the conference, but our partying had made it difficult to explore other restaurants and still get to the club or venue we wanted early enough to avoid waiting in long lines. I'd missed out on the fun at the Marquee Friday night, so I knew I had to make the best out of Saturday's outing. Yet, for some reason, the idea of clubbing was no longer as exciting it had been days ago.

MGM's ballroom had been transformed from a massive meeting room into an elegant reception area. Circular tables with white tablecloths and lit silver, cylinder candles decorated each table. A deejay was stationed near the center of the room and there was a large dance floor area in front of him. I watched him bounce to the beat as he switched one gospel song for another. He mixed a diversity of Christian music from Contemporary to Holy Hip Hop. As much as I would have loved to have run out on the dance floor and rocked to Tye Tribbitt's "Stayed On You," I resisted the urge. It just didn't seem right to dance to a song about keeping my mind stayed on Jesus, then two hours later be at XS dancing to a song about wearing Apple Bottom jeans, boots with the fur, and getting low, low, low, low, low, low, low.

Eventually, Sky and I made our way over to Nelson and Owen. I'd been feeling awkward around Nelson ever since our dispute on Thursday night. I was getting the strong feeling that Nelson genuinely liked me. Not the wanna-be player Nelson, but the funny, charming Nelson who I actually could stomach being around for more than five minutes. I was flattered by his interest, but I wasn't so sure about pursuing anything more than friendship with him. He was my best friend's husband's brother which made it too Hallmark movie-like for us to end up together. This wasn't a Debbie Macomber novel, this was real life, and in real life, best friends didn't end up in romantic relationships with brothers.

I also didn't trust Nelson. Yeah, he might have more than one side to him, but the part of him that believed it was okay to dog women out scared me. Why would I knowingly get involved with a self-professed ladies' man? Now, that wouldn't be using the brain God gave me.

My final issue had nothing to do with Nelson and a lot to do with myself. My career was everything to me and at that moment, it was falling apart. There was no way that I could date Nelson, Larry, or any other guy for that matter. Since my promotion issue, I hadn't even hung out with Clyde—my old faithful, something-to-do guy back in Atlanta. I had to keep my focus on what I could control. Loving men had a way of making the most sensible and intelligent woman lose her marbles. Take Amber for example. As much as I understood her marriage, there were times when dealing with Eric drove her so nutty that she said and did some disturbing things. I can't imagine going through the ups and downs of a relationship while at the same time having to deal with the ups and downs of my career. Many women have asked the question, can I have it all? In my opinion, the answer is no. I'm trying to one day be the superintendent of schools in my district. I'll never make it to my dream if I allow loving some man to cloud my judgment.

"Hey, guys," Sky said to Nelson and Owen when we were within close range of them.

"Don't you all look nice in your sports jackets," I said, sweetly.

"And you ladies look fabulous as always," Owen said.

"I agree. You all look very nice," Nelson said.

"Why are you two still eating? After all that fried rice they gave us, I won't be able to eat anything until lunch tomorrow," I said in an attempt to steer the conversation away from how nice we all looked.

"Hey, we're growing men. We need nourishment," Owen joked.

"The only place you two are growing is those big bellies," Sky kidded.

We all laughed as Owen stuck out his gut and rubbed his belly.

"I can't believe that this time tomorrow we'll be back home. As much as I miss my family and friends, I'm really going to miss you guys," Sky said.

We all nodded and thought about her statement. In such a short time, we had formed a bond, a friendship. In a matter of hours, we would be going home as if this whole experience never happened. It was sad to think about leaving, but we each had a life to live and staying in Vegas wasn't an option.

"Since we have to go tomorrow, come rain or shine, let's go out with a bang. Y'all ready to hit The Strip?" Nelson asked.

I shrugged. "I'm ready when you are."

Nelson

The people who owned XS had to be out of their minds. Yes, it was probably the most popular club in Las Vegas. This was evident by the line that was longer than any club line I'd ever seen—and we had gotten there early. Our plan was to wait in the ridiculous line to see what all of the fuss was about, but after standing there for twenty minutes, we found out that the cover charge was $20 for women, but $50 for men!

Owen and I quickly exited the line. We had paid some exorbitant prices while in Vegas for food and other activities, but that was the last draw. Outside of feeding myself, I refused to spend another dime in this city.

Sky and Tisha agreed that the price for men was way too high and decided to opt out of clubbing for the night with us. It was our last night in Vegas and we'd actually walked away from the party. Who would have thought that a cover charge would have stopped our fun? I would have liked to pretend that we'd each grown a big enough conscious during the conference to quit partying based on the messages we'd received alone, but that would have been untrue. I chuckled to myself later as I thought about how God could use anything to get our attention, even exorbitant club prices.

Instead of heading immediately back to the MGM, we decided to walk the Las Vegas Strip a bit and take in the night attractions like the volcanic waterfalls at the Mirage and the sinking pirate ship at Treasure Island. We truly were having a blast without the whole club scene when Sky fell and sprained her ankle. Owen and I helped her up, but it was evident that she needed medical attention. There was a medical center at the MGM that the conference attendees had access to so we agreed Sky needed to get there right away. We all were about to usher her back to the MGM Grand when she stopped Tisha and I.

"Owen can take me back to the hotel. You two stay and enjoy The Strip," she said.

"What?" Tisha asked, incredulously. "We're not going to stay here while you're hurt."

"I don't want you to come," Sky persisted.

Tisha gasped. "Why not?"

"Because this is your last night in Vegas, and even though the two of you live in Atlanta, I know you're never going to have this chance again if you don't take it now," Sky said.

I was confused, so I asked, "What are you talking about? What chance?"

"The chance to spend some quality time together without a zillion people around. The chance to get to know each other. The chance to fall in love. You two like each other, but you're both too stupid to do anything about it. So I'm going to do it for you. Tisha and Nelson, neither of you are allowed to go back with me to the hotel. Owen and I are leaving. We'll catch a cab back to the hotel. You guys are on your own," Sky said.

Owen shrugged like he was just following orders and helped Sky limp away from us. Tisha and I stared at their backs for about a minute before turning to face each other.

"What was that all about?" I asked.

"That right there is what you call a set-up," Tisha said then laughed.

"I believe you're right. So, what do we do about it?" I asked.

"Normally, I would tell Sky off and go with her anyway, but it is our last night and I'm not ready to go inside just yet," she said.

"Me neither," I said. "You want to keep walking?"

"Yeah. A walk sounds nice."

Lesson 20: Look Up for Your Blessings

Every good gift and every perfect gift is from above.
(James 1:17)

Tisha

Nelson and I stayed out, walking the Las Vegas Strip and talking, all night long. When the sun began to rise, we went to breakfast at a cheap buffet inside of Circus Circus. I was extremely comfortable being alone with him. I wasn't worried about him pushing up on me or trying to make me do something I wasn't ready for. Nelson was very respectful and handled me with care. If I had to place a bet on Nelson's character five days ago, I would have lost, big time.

After breakfast, we caught a cab back to the MGM Grand. We would have walked, but we'd thoughtlessly traveled almost three miles up The Strip and weren't willing to take the long hike back. Arriving at our hotel within minutes, Nelson ushered me to my room. I opened the door and peeked inside to make sure Sky was in her bed and not down in the medical center, or even worse, at a hospital. She was wrapped up tightly under the thick, white comforter, snoring away. I giggled and closed the door so that she wouldn't hear our noise in the hallway.

"Thank you, Nelson, for one of the best nights out in my life. All of that clubbing and partying we did over the last several days was really stupid. I had much more fun just relaxing with you than trying to shut down the club," I said.

"I know. I came to Las Vegas thinking I was going to paint the town red. I thought the L.V.P.D. was going to have to lock me up just to get me to calm down. But who knew having a good time could really be as simple as just spending time with someone you care about?" he asked.

I fidgeted. Our conversation was getting awkward quickly. "I probably better go and start getting my bags packed. We still have the Singles class at 10 o'clock and I haven't even begun to put my clothes back into the suitcase."

"Yeah, me too. I need to go pack, I mean," he said. "I guess I'll see you in a little while."

"Okay," I said.

Nelson stepped closer to me and titled my chin upwards toward him. I knew he planned to kiss me, and somewhere deep inside me a voice screamed "run," but my feet remained glued to the ground. He bent down and planted the most sincere kiss on my lips that I have ever experienced. His lips lingered for a moment, but then he withdrew himself from me, winked, and walked down the hallway away from me.

I wasn't sure if the whole incident was premeditated, but I found myself feeling overwhelmed by the romantic moment. It felt really good to be with him, but as I watched him grow smaller and smaller as he moved further away, I was sure of one thing—I had to get Nelson Hayes out of my system immediately. He was a player at heart, I was on the fast track to my dream career, we were both headed back to Atlanta later in the day, and ultimately, a relationship between us would never work.

Martin read James 1:17 from the Amplified Bible to us aloud. "Every good gift and every perfect, free, large, and full gift is from above; it comes down from the Father of all that gives light, in the shining of Whom there can be no variation—rising or setting—or shadow cast by His turning—as in an eclipse.

"Thank you all for sticking with us through this conference. As we prepare to close this event, we leave you all with this final verse, James chapter one, verse 17. We've given you so much to chew on in these five Singles 101 classes, and to cap it off, it is important that you know this final message—everything that is good comes from God. Anything that you want in this life that is a good thing, God has it. If you want marriage, God has it. If you want a great career, it's in God's hands. If you want children or even just a closer walk with Him, He can do it. This is why you count it all joy when trials come into your life. You can have joy because you realize that God has all that you need to overcome that trial and that He will give it to you as a free gift. I say free because sometimes when people give us something valuable it isn't free. They'll be your friend as long as you . . . They'll give you that job if you just . . . They will even marry you if you would simply . . . There's always a catch, always a condition to the gift. But God isn't a shady gift giver. He doesn't wait until you're so desperate for the gift that you'll agree to do anything for it and then say, 'Gotcha!' Nope. Instead He'll push you beyond desperation until you get to a place where patience has had its way in your life and you can say with honesty, 'Whatever Your will, Lord, is alright with me.' In the midst of your joy, your single-mindedness, your humility, your choice of eternal life, He will give you the free gift of salvation. But it doesn't stop there. He will endow you with whatever it is that you need. Good gift, perfect gifts. Don't you see that His plan was always to bless you? It was always for your good even in the hardest moments. He never forgot about you; He just wanted to give you the very best. And now you're ready. You can handle His favor. It's not going to ruin you or spoil you.

"For those of you who are parents, you know how sometimes you have to intentionally withhold items from your children so that the item won't spoil them. Yeah, you could afford to buy them a new car for their sweet sixteenth birthday, but you know they couldn't handle it, so you wait until they are twenty-one. They've walked, taken the bus, caught rides, saved up a little money, and now you can give them the car they wanted because it won't be too much. It's a good gift now. A good gift given at a bad time can quickly become a bad gift. But God only hands out good gifts, so the timing has got to be right."

Lydia stepped next to her husband and said, "Before we part ways from you, we want to give you all a gift. It's not valuable to the untrained eye, but to you, it will be a good gift because you will understand its relevance."

She took a palm sized, tan rock out of a bag and held it up in the air. "As you leave this room, you will each be given one of these rocks. Yes, a stone. This rock symbolizes a piece of a mountain. These rocks were gathered from the Spring Mountains out here in Nevada.

"The Bible says that if you tell a mountain to move and have the faith of a mustard seed, it will move. We've talked about activating your faith and believing in God when you make your requests known to him. Every time you look at this rock, I want you to remember that you are a mountain mover. With faith in God, all things are possible for you. Receive the good gifts He has in store for you by believing in Him. Let us end with a word of prayer."

Everyone bowed their heads and closed their eyes as Martin prayed for us all. "Heavenly Father, we thank You for a successful and safe singles conference. We thank You for every person that has come to this event expecting mountains to be moved in their lives. As they travel to their homes, we asked for Your traveling grace and mercy. Help them not to forget the many lessons they have learned, but to hold tight to all of the words You have spoken into their lives. Change their hearts and attitudes toward You. Let them choose You over any temptation this world has to offer. When they find themselves in the midst of trials, remind them to be joyful, for you are with them and shall use the most difficult circumstances in their lives to bring out the very best in them. Show them how to activate their faith so that every mountain in their life will be moved and cast into the sea. We receive Your blessings with a single mind, in the name of Jesus Christ. Amen."

Lesson 21: What's It Gonna Be?

And if it seem evil unto you to serve the LORD, choose you this day whom ye will serve; whether the gods which your fathers served that *were* on the other side of the flood, or the gods of the Amorites, in whose land ye dwell: but as for me and my house, we will serve the LORD. (Joshua: 24:15)

Tisha

I changed my return flight. We were scheduled to depart from Las Vegas' McCarran Airport at 4:30 p.m., but I took the 3:00 p.m. flight to Atlanta, dishing out $150 for the change fee. I couldn't face Nelson. My mind was whirling with everything I'd learned at the conference and my career concerns. Adding Nelson to the pot of confusion called my life was not an option. Before I left, I hugged Sky and Owen goodbye and told them to keep in touch. I informed Amber about my plans to take the earlier flight, tucked my souvenir rock into my purse, and took a cab to the airport.

Yep, after all of the inspirational lessons about faith and moving mountains, I chose to run home afraid.

Lena

I didn't want that stupid rock! The minute we got back to the room, I gave my rock to Jessica. She tried to convince me to keep it, but for what? My trip was a bust for the most part. I barely got to see Eric, I never got a chance to party, I cut off my relationship with Douglass, and Amber had spent my money and outsmarted me. I was just glad to go home, hug my daughter, and get back to planning her birthday party—if I could even afford it after all of the money I'd lost gambling.

I noticed that Tisha was on the same flight as me on the way back home. I wasn't sure why she wasn't with Amber, Eric, and Nelson, but I also didn't care. As the plane ascended into the air, I found myself thinking about Douglass and what Dr. Wilson had said about the right one not being perfect, but being perfect for me. Possibly I was too harsh with him. Perhaps it was worth giving a relationship with him another try. Maybe I'd give him a call when I got back to Atlanta. Mmm, maybe I wouldn't.

Nelson

Tisha left without saying goodbye. I felt like I'd been sucker punched when Amber explained to me that Tisha had taken an earlier flight. Not the one to get all emotional, I pretended not to care, but deep down, I was injured. How could she let me kiss her and then just act as if it meant nothing at all to her? I was certain when I left her that morning that it was the beginning of something special between us. It wouldn't be the first time that I was wrong.

Sky and Owen tried to reassure me about Tisha, but I accepted it for what it was—some weird form of a vacationship.

They meant well, but from that point on, my life would be much easier if I let Tisha go and moved on. What happens in Vegas, stays in Vegas, right?

On the way back through the McCarran Airport, I ignored the slot machines. Nothing that mattered five days ago seemed important now. While waiting for our flight to start boarding, I eyed the stone that the Woods had given to us. Nearly a week in Las Vegas and all I was returning home with was two new friends, a wounded heart, and a rock from the middle of the desert.

July

Lesson 22: Go Get It

And from the days of John the Baptist until now the kingdom of heaven suffereth violence, and the violent take it by force. (Matthew 11:12)

Tisha

By July, I had narrowed down my choices. Starting my own charter school or moving on to a new career were out of the question. I enjoyed my career in education, yet I wasn't ready to take on the responsibility of entrepreneurship. As far as I was concerned, I only had two options: leave DeKalb County School District and find a position elsewhere, or fight tooth and nail for the promotion I deserved. Although I really wanted to stay in my current district, I was beginning to lean in the direction of walking away. I had updated my resume and had begun job searching in other counties. There were a few comparable job opportunities in the surrounding counties of Rockdale, Fulton, and Gwinnett, but my heart broke every time I seriously thought about the transition. Nevertheless, I submitted applications to them all, just in case it was really time to let go.

I knew that it seemed silly that I would continue to hold on to a school district that wanted to keep me stagnant, but sometimes, when you've worked hard and invested a great deal into a person, place, or thing, you just want to see it through to the very bitter end. I almost felt as if my district was a long-term relationship with a man I really loved who didn't want to fully commit. Maybe that was one of the reasons I didn't want to get involved with Nelson—I was already involved with my career.

I was in the process of hoping for the best, but bracing for the worst when I received the phone call that I'd been dreading. Another principal in the district, Chandra, who appeared to always know the scoop down at the Board of Education, called me up around the first of the month.

"Girl!" she exclaimed before I could give her the customary phone greeting.

"Hey, Chandra. What's going on?"

"You are *never* going believe this mess. If I didn't hear it from a reliable source, I wouldn't believe it either. I mean, I know that the BOE does some outlandish stuff sometimes, but this right here is for the birds."

I usually try not to get caught up in Chandra's hearsay and gossip, but with my work-related concerns, I knew I had to keep my ear to the streets. "What? You're killing me over here? What happened? What did you hear?"

"They hired someone for the regional superintendent position, and unfortunately, it isn't you," she said, matter-of-factly.

My heart plummeted. "What? Who? Who'd they hire?"

I could hear her lips smack as if she was just as offended by the news as I. "That's where it gets even more ridiculous. The woman's name is Margret Hill. She's from outside the district. I heard she's from up North, New Jersey, I believe. But get this, she only has three years of experience as a principal and she's only taught in the classroom for four years before that. This woman only has a total of seven years in education. Seven! Haven't you been working in the field for fourteen years?"

"Fifteen," I said, dryly.

"See, now, that's just cold. Not only did they hire externally when they had qualified candidates internally, but they also hired someone who is less qualified than others, like yourself, who applied for the job. I am so speechless about the situation. That was dirty. Who does this kind of thing?"

"Obviously, DeKalb County School District," I replied, feeling disgruntled. For someone who was speechless, Chandra sure had a lot to say. She continued to rant and rave in my ear for another ten minutes about the unfair practices of our employer. I held the phone and half-listened, half-zoned out. What was I going to do? My district was making a fool out of me and anyone else who was up for the promotion but didn't get it. Why had we been overlooked? Why were the superintendent and school board so determined to maintain status quo while bringing in under-qualified candidates?

As Chandra rambled, I took odds and ends from what she told me and conducted an internet search on Margaret Hill. Sure enough, she'd only been working in education for a little over seven years, up in Camden, New Jersey. I located her Facebook page in which she's recently posted a status update that she'd been hired as a regional superintendent and was relocating to Georgia. Her post had ninety-eight likes and numerous congratulations. Immediately, I felt sick to my stomach.

By the time I hung up with Chandra, I was throwing-up, literally. My head was spinning. I realized that something like this could occur, but now that it had, it was more devastating than I had prepared for. My mind swarmed with thoughts about my next move.

Pray you get one of those jobs with another county.

Call the superintendent and give him a piece of your mind.

Maybe you should move out of state.

You might want to revisit that idea of forming a charter school.

Take the job at Ponce De Leon Alternative High School.

Just go back to your old job at Turner Hill. It wasn't a bad position. You can always try again next year.

Next year? That was definitely not an option. No. As much as I felt lower than I've been in a really long time, I would not sit still and return to my old job. It was time for change, and one way or another, my position would be changing for the better.

I quickly dressed, jumped into my car, and drove over to Amber's house. My friend answered the door looking just as crazed as I suspected I did.

"Good, you're here," Amber said, motioning for me to enter into the house. "I was just about to call you."

I stood at the door, gazing at Amber quizzically. Had the news spread that fast? What, were they announcing it on the morning show or in the paper? "You were? How did you find out?"

"That's a stupid question. How do you think I found out?"

"It's not a stupid question. I didn't know you knew? I just found out myself, but how did you find out before I did?"

Amber rolled her eyes. "First of all, come inside and stop letting my air conditioning out of the house."

"Oh," I said before walking into the house and closing the door behind me.

She led me to the living room, and we sat down on her plush sofa. "Second, I have a feeling that we're not talking about the same thing. I'm referring to me finding out that I'm pregnant again," she said, pointing to herself. "What are *you* talking about?"

I instantly scanned her stomach which appeared normal. No baby bump from what I could see. "You're pregnant? For real? How pregnant?"

She gave me a sneaky grin. "About a month. I guess we enjoyed Vegas a little too much."

I laughed. "I guess what happens in Vegas doesn't always stay there."

"Ain't that the truth," she said.

Yes, Amber was a married woman, but I had just gotten used to her having one child and a step-kid. She was working on another addition to the family and I couldn't even slow down long enough to have a relationship that lasted longer than six months. "So, what . . . how does Eric feel about it? Are you okay with it?"

"Eric almost passed out when I told him after my doctor's appointment this morning. It's not that he has a problem with us having another child, but we're still trying to get a grasp on being E. J.'s parents, and now, if it all works out, we will be parents to this baby, too. Me? I want another kid and I guess at my age it's best to just have all I'm going to have at once, but it's just a surprise. I struggled with having the first child and now, bam! I'm pregnant again."

I looked around her tastefully decorated living room. I remembered when Amber first bought that house years ago and we spent countless hours shopping for furniture, window treatments, and the perfect neutral color of paint for her living room walls. "Well, if you all keep having babies, you're going to have to move into a bigger house."

"No, we won't! This place is paid for. I'm not going anywhere," she said with too much attitude. I couldn't decipher if the pregnancy hormones had already kicked in or if Amber was just being her usual, mildly grumpy self. She sighed loudly and said, "So if you weren't talking about my pregnancy, what were you talking about?"

For a moment, my crisis had been forgotten, disregarded by Amber's pregnancy news. I had actually appreciated the distraction; it calmed me for a few minutes. But with Amber's question, the queasiness in my gut returned. "The BOE. They gave the job I wanted to someone else from out of state who doesn't have even half of my qualifications."

"Seriously? Are you sure?"

"Yep. Another principal called me today and told me."

"Who? Chandra?"

"Who else?"

"Then it's true. Chandra might be the biggest gossip I've ever seen, but everything she says always turns out to be the truth."

"You're right. Amber, I'm so disappointed. I knew that something like this was likely to happen, but I was really hoping that Dr. Cooper would change his mind and do the right thing. I feel like my world has just fallen apart. What am I going to do? I can't see myself going back to Turner Hill, or even worse, going to Ponce De Leon. I'm not going to accept backtracking in my career. It looks like I'll have to get a job with another district which I really didn't want to have to do." I felt tears well up in my eyes as I verbalized my thoughts to my best friend.

Amber peered at me with unsympathetic eyes. It was the last response I'd expected from her.

"Why are you looking at me like that? Didn't you hear what I just said? They're crushing my dreams!" I said, becoming more angered by the moment.

Amber poked her lips out at me. At that second, I realized that she was about to tell me off.

"Yes, I heard everything you just said, and you sound like a spoiled brat."

"What?"

"You heard me. Spoiled. 'They're crushing my dreams,'" she mocked me. "The Tisha I know would never let anyone keep her away from her dreams—not Dr. Cooper, or the BOE, or the entire state of Georgia. I hope you didn't come over here thinking that I was going to coddle you. The only person I'm coddling is upstairs, taking a nap in his crib. Now, they gave the position to someone else. Is it fair? No, but it's done. The question is, what are you going to do about it? Are you going to decide that it's time to cut your losses and move on to a place where you can be valued? Are you going to choose to make your own rules and start your own school? Or are you going to stand up for yourself and make them give you the promotion you deserve? Those are your only three choices, the only three options that the Tisha I know would even consider. But whichever you choose, you're not going to sit up in my living room wallowing and feeling bad for yourself—not when you just came home from a life-changing singles conference and have already been told that your faith has the ability to move mountains. Don't let it just be another feel-good Bible verse. Apply it to your life and go get your dreams."

I stared at Amber feeling stunned. I'd come over her house searching for a shoulder to cry on and maybe a small pep talk, but Amber had just hit me over my head with a super-sized dose of the truth. She was right. It wasn't time to complain, mope, or be discouraged. Although I had a right to feel saddened by my circumstances, feeling down has never resolved anyone's problems. I could waste time blaming the BOE and trash-talking them about my promotion, or I could get up and go get it for myself. I really didn't know why I ever put my success in someone else's hands to begin with. My dreams were dependent on myself and God. No one else had the privilege of deciding how high I could go.

"Okay, that came out a bit rough, but I get your point," I finally said to Amber. "And, you're right. I'm a fighter, not a complainer. I can't let this situation stop me from pursuing my goals or make me feel like a failure."

"That's what I'm talking about," Amber said, wearing a serious expression. "So what's the plan?"

Good question. A part of me felt like telling the entire county to kick rocks, but was I really ready to leave behind all of my hard work? "The plan is . . . the plan is . . . the plan is to appeal the school board's decision. I know that the easy route would be to simply leave, but I just can't without at least trying to get them to making it right with me. I know I'm being stubborn about this, but if I just walk away with my tail tucked between my legs, I'll regret it and always wonder what would have happened if I would have fought against their decision."

Amber nodded slowly. "I understand. How do you intend to fight it?"

I scratched my head, thinking. Any moves I made would have to be implemented quickly and strategically. We were already halfway through the summer. If I wanted a promotion, I would have to act now. "I don't know. There's a school board meeting this coming Monday and I can address them at the meeting."

"Will addressing them at the board meeting alone work?" Amber asked.

"Probably not, but it will at least let them know how serious I am and it will inform the community about their unfair employment practices."

"Alright. What else can you do?"

My mind went blank for a few seconds. I was just a high school principal. How could I go against the decision of a school board and expect to win? Then it hit me. I couldn't, but I knew some people who could. "I can make a few phone calls, get some allies. I've built relationships with some powerful people over the years like the mayors of Decatur, Lithonia, and Atlanta, as well as a few congressmen and one of the senators. I'm pretty sure if I contacted them and made them aware of my circumstances, they would at least be willing to write letters on my behalf, strongly urging the district to reconsider. I can also contact a lawyer and see if I have any legal rights."

Amber smiled, finally. "Now, that's the Tisha I know. Call Sherri Greene. She did a great job handling Eric's custody case. I'm sure she could help you or at least point you to an attorney who can."

I nodded and took out my cell phone. "Good idea. I'm starting to feel better already. Thanks so much for keeping it real with me and not just letting me throw a pity party."

Amber reached out and covered one of my hands with her own. "Trust me when I say that I used to be the pity party queen, but over the last handful of years, God has had to have those same tough talks with me, using the people closest to me as His mouthpiece. It didn't feel good to hear the truth, but the truth did set me free. So, get to work. You have a lot of work to do and only a few days to get it done. In the meantime, I'm going to go check on my baby and call my mother to tell her about the new addition to the family."

In three business days, I managed to contact my political associates and secure their assistance. I also met with Sherri Greene to discuss legal options, and I had contacted the BOE and requested to be on the upcoming meeting's agenda to present my case. Because of the in-depth nature of my concern, I had been scheduled to present at the board's work session, held Monday afternoon, and if a vote was deemed necessary, also attend the evening board business meeting. By Monday, I was both energized and anxious. I believed that I had enough support to make the board pay attention to me. I only hoped that it wasn't too late to get them to change their minds.

I'd also received a response from Gwinnett County, scheduling an interview with me for the Thursday after my board meeting appearance. If my appeal didn't go well, at least there was an opportunity to move on.

When I walked into the board's work session fifteen minutes early with Amber and Sherri by my side, I was sweating bullets. Both the work session and business meeting were held at the Robert R. Freeman Administrative & Instructional Complex in Stone Mountain, Georgia. A few of the board members who were already there eyed me suspiciously, but it wasn't as if I didn't expect a little hostility. I was certain that letters on my behalf from my politician friends had streamed into their email inboxes and mailboxes. I had seven of the most influential people in the state of Georgia backing me—the BOE underestimated me if they thought I would come alone or not at all. By the way Dr. Cooper looked at me when he saw me in the room, I was certain he was one of those who were doing the underestimating.

Previous to that day, I rarely participated in school board meetings; as a principal, I was too busy running my school than keeping up with monthly BOE meetings. When the meeting begun, I wished I had attended more often to have a better handle on what to expect and how to best present my case. I was somewhat relieved when they allowed me to speak early in the session. I was so nervous that waiting for my turn amongst all of their other business was pure torture.

I knew that I had a limited amount of time to speak, so I quickly distributed to the group my curriculum vitae, along with three letter of recommendation from educators, and my seven letters of support from the politicians. I explained how I had applied for the position of regional superintendent, but had been re-directed to overseeing a failing alternative high school, and how the position that I wanted was possibly given to someone with half of my qualifications. I requested that the board reconsider my request for promotion, and I notified them of my intention to leave the district if I was demoted to Ponce De Leon or sent back to Turner Hill High.

"I'm not asking for anything that I do not deserve," I said during the session. "I've worked faithfully for this district for fifteen years, always believing that if I excelled in my duties that I would be rewarded with positive results from my school and students, as well as opportunities to advance within the district. I am extremely disappointed that a work ethic like my own is not valued here in DeKalb, and that instead of utilizing the best within the system, the board would seek outsiders who are not familiar with our schools and students, nor as qualified, to come in and be promoted over diligent employees like myself. Yet, even though I am saddened by the way I've been treated and it would probably be easier to just leave the district, I am here with you all today because I love this district and I'm willing to give it another chance. I live in this county, I bought a house in this county, and I want to see my tax dollars well used in this county. Instead of complaining like some do about the state of our educational system, I am committed to being a part of the solution. With my promotion, I will be in an even better position to influence positive change and growth within our county. If I am denied, I won't give up my fight for improvement, but unfortunately, another county will reap the benefits of my passion, drive, and expertise. So I ask you today to make the right decision and reconsider me for regional superintendent."

By the time I took my seat, I was both depleted and exhilarated. I had spoken the truth and not held back. I had stood up for myself and demonstrated my very best. I decided at that moment that if the BOE couldn't see the benefit of keeping me around, they didn't deserve me. I would no longer hold on to the district if they disregarded me—I was ready and willing to let go. My next step was in God's hands and whatever path He led me down, I would follow.

The board discussed the matter thoroughly in my presence. It was quickly evident that although most of them agreed that I should be promoted, a few did not. In addition, Margret Hill had already been hired for the opening of regional superintendent, had already received her offer of employment, and had already signed her work contract. Even if they wanted to replace her for me, it was now a legal and ethical issue. Technically, the state of Georgia was a Right to Work state, meaning that an employer could fire an employee at any time and for any reason, and it was completely legal. But just because firing could happen, didn't mean it should, or that the fired employee could not cause a ruckus or pursue legal action. On this premise, Margret's employment was basically written in stone, at least for a year.

In my mind, I was about to give up when one of the board members suggested a different position for me. There was an unfilled position as the Executive Director of Leadership which was a senior level administrative position that had just opened up at the end of the school year. The person who was previously in the position had an ongoing health condition that had progressively become worse. His wife had been begging him to quit, but he refused to do so until he was hospitalized in May for three weeks. The doctors basically told him that if he didn't quit his job and take it easy, he wouldn't live to see another birthday.

The executive director of leadership reported to the same person as regional superintendents—the deputy superintendent. If given the job, it would be a promotion that would increase my salary substantially and would still put me in the same job tier as those who were regional superintendents. It would also grant me the opportunity to impact the district in a greater manner because I wouldn't just be dealing with a particular region of schools, I would have access to administrators at all of the schools in the district. I had to admit, it was the perfect position for me.

The board agreed to vote on me being placed in the position at the board meeting that evening. I had already been placed on the agenda as a provision in case there needed to be a vote, so all was in order to expedite the matter. I walked out of the session feeling overwhelmed by God's sovereignty. Could it be that I was passed over for the regional superintendent job because He had an even better position in store for me?

As much as I was thrilled about the new opportunity that was set before me, I didn't allow myself to get too excited. Until they officially voted and the vote was in favor of giving the job to me, the matter still was unresolved. I truly believed that the position was mine, and I felt God's hand of favor upon my life, but I would remain open to all outcomes until the deal was finalized.

That evening at 7:45 p.m., the board addressed my item on the agenda. I sat next to Amber, squeezing her hand as the board's chair provided an overview of the matter and allowed for questions. When no questions were asked, the item was submitted for a vote. I closed my eyes the moment the vote was raised, not wanting to see any of their faces as they made their final decision. When I heard all "ayes" and no "nays," a ton of weight fell from my shoulders. The decision was unanimous—I would be the new executive director of leadership.

I almost stood up and danced a jig, but I held my composure, engaged in a fist bump with Amber, and offered God a silent thank you.

The meeting was adjourned forty minutes later, and after accepting congratulations from a few well-wishers, Amber and I headed for the door. I was almost to the exit, when I looked up and saw Eric standing by the door next to his brother, Nelson. I had no clue either of them had come to the meeting in support of me. I hadn't spoken to Nelson since the Vegas trip. There was no way he could have known about the BOE meeting unless Eric or Amber had told him. I looked at Amber who smiled brightly and turned my attention to Eric who attempted to quickly look away, and instantly knew the real deal. I had been set up, again.

Lesson 23: What Do Your Words & Actions Say About You?

For every tree is known by his own fruit... A good man out of the good treasure of his heart bringeth forth that which is good; and an evil man out of the evil treasure of his heart bringeth forth that which is evil: for of the abundance of the heart his mouth speaketh. (Luke 6:44-45)

Nelson

I wasn't certain about many things in life, but I was sure about Tisha—I had to have her. Ever since the Vegas trip I'd been thinking about her nonstop. That was major for me because one thing I never did was obsess over a woman. Charmaine was the only female who had ever caused me to pine over her. When she broke my heart 25 years ago, I promised myself I would never chase after another woman, and I certainly wouldn't fall in love again. Since then I'd been true to my pledge, treating women as mere trophies rather than potential companions. To me, women were predictable, replaceable, and incapable of earning my trust. I had this extreme fear that if I let a woman in my heart, the result would be similar to Charmaine—I would end up played. So instead, I did the playing, and it worked well for me, until those five days in Vegas with Tisha.

It almost felt divine the way I made amends with Charmaine right before I went to the conference and spent time with Tisha, as if God knew me forgiving Charmaine would open me up for a relationship with someone else. The only problem was that right when I was emotionally available for the first time in my life since college, the one person that I wanted to give my heart to was emotionally a hot mess. Ironic indeed.

I tried to contact Tisha numerous times once we got back to Atlanta, but she ignored all of my calls. I even tried to camp out at Eric's house a few times, hoping she would stop by to see Amber, but she never did—at least while I was there. Unfortunately, I didn't have her address or I would have dropped by her place. I tried to get the address from Amber, but she told me if I popped up unannounced and uninvited, it would only make me look like a stalker. She was probably right. I had a chick do that to me once and it was really weird. So, before I completely ruined my chances with her, I dropped the idea of Googling her address.

A month had passed and I was beginning to lose hope that I would ever see her again when Amber and Eric showed up at my doorstep. I owned a three-bedroom luxury condo in Atlanta, off Glenwood Avenue, and a buddy of mine, Sean, rented a room from me, which helped me keep up with the mortgage. I was giving Sean a terrible beat down on the Madden football video game when the Hayes clan came pounding on my door. They entered the house, Amber carrying my nephew E. J. and Jonelle following closely behind her father.

"What's this?" I asked. "Y'all brought the *whole* family? Did someone die?"

"No, everyone's alive . . . I think," Amber said, putting E. J. on the floor. The boy wasted no time walking over to the game system and hitting the eject button.

"No!" I yelled, but it was too late. My beat down of Sean was forever lost.

"E. J.," Amber said, correctively. "I'm sorry, Nelson."

"Thanks, E. J.," Sean said, snickering. "I guess we will never know who would have won that game."

"Sorry about your game, man, but we have more important matters to talk to you about," Eric said.

I pouted. "What's more important than raking this loser, Sean, over the coals on Madden?"

"Tisha."

The minute I heard her name come out of my brother's mouth, my progress on Madden disappeared from my mind.

"What's wrong with Tisha?" I asked.

"She's decided to take on the Board of Education about that promotion she was so hung up on during the Vegas trip," Amber said. "They gave the promotion to someone else, someone less qualified."

"That's messed up. But what does that have to do with me?"

"You've been trying to get her attention ever since the trip. Here's your chance to win her over," Eric said.

"Okay, I'm not following you. What does her job problem have to do with me?"

"You said yourself that she wouldn't open herself up to you because she was so consumed with this promotion. Maybe if you showed some interest in her career, if you supported her in her fight to get this promotion, she'll change her mind about being with you," Eric said.

I started to understand where Eric was going with the conversation, but I wasn't sure it would actually work. I looked over at Amber who also seemed convinced that this was the right move. Being her best friend, Amber would know what would work and what wouldn't. If Amber thought it was a good idea, I would have to consider it.

"Amber," I said. "Do you really believe Tisha wants my support on this? She was pretty clear that she didn't want me in her life. I've tried to call her and everything, but she's completely ignoring me. I don't want to go out of my way to be there for her and then she just blow me off again."

"Nelson," Amber began, "I can't promise you that she'll come running back into your arms. Tisha is a real piece of work and she's not the easiest person to deal with, but you already know that. But she really needs the people who care about her to have her back right now. I really believe that if you show up for her now when so much is on the line, she won't take it lightly and she certainly won't forget it."

"I guess, I'm willing to give it a try. But what can I do?"

"You just have to be there," Amber said. "She's meeting with the board on Monday. Just come to the meeting. Your presence alone will speak volumes."

"And bring a small bouquet of flowers," Eric said.

"Flowers?"

Eric added, "If she wins, it will be like congratulations flowers, but if she loses, the flowers might help make her feel better. I'm telling you, man. Flowers go a long way with women."

Sean nodded. "Your brother's right. Anytime I'm in the doghouse with my woman, I buy her flowers. Works almost every time, especially if you send them to her job. Women like showing off in front of their coworkers."

"What?" Amber asked. "So is that your theory behind flowers, Eric? All those time you bought me flowers, were you just trying to dig your way out of the doghouse?"

"Babe, that's not what I said. I was saying that flowers would help, but Sean said that flowers—"

I interrupted before the conversation turned ugly. "Amber, I need you to focus. This discussion is about what I need to do to get Tisha back, not you and my brother and why he bought you flowers. So, getting back to me, my question to you is should I get her flowers?"

Amber bit her lip, seemingly upset that she couldn't grill my brother about his flower giving. "Maybe," she said finally.

"Maybe?" I asked.

"Okay, yes. Yes! Yes! Yes! Women, we love getting flowers—well most of us do. It makes us feel important and loved. Flowers, especially certain kinds like orchards, are not cheap. So when a man gives us flowers it's like he is saying that he is willing to invest his hard earned money into making us smile. But now that I've said that, Eric, the next time you bring me flowers, it better be the biggest, most beautiful bouquet I've ever seen."

Eric grumbled. "See what you all have caused in my marriage?"

"You brought that on yourself, bro. You're the one who mentioned flowers. But I get the point you all are trying to make. Be at the meeting, bring flowers, and show her that I support her."

"You've got it, man."

"Okay, okay. So, which one of you are going to give me some money to get these flowers? Like Amber said, they aren't cheap. After spending all of my money in Vegas, I'm going to need a loan for these flowers."

Sean walked out of the room. Amber and Eric looked at each other. I assume they were communicating nonverbally through their eyes because a few seconds later, Amber began heading for the door, and Eric said, "It's time for us to go. Kids, come on. Say goodbye to Uncle Nelson."

A couple days later, I sat in the back of the board meeting watching Tisha carefully. Eric had picked me up and brought me with him to the meeting so that Tisha wouldn't know I was coming. I tightened my grip around the half dozen bouquet of yellow roses I had purchased for her. It wasn't until I felt the prick of one of the thorns that I eased up. It bothered me to watch the woman that I cared so deeply for sit stoically and await such a crucial decision. I could tell that it was eating her up on the inside. Each time she turned to whisper to Amber—which she did often—I could see the side of her face and it was void of expression. I had begun to figure out that Tisha wore her emotions in her eyes. She was good at appearing as if nothing was affecting her, but her eyes told a different story. She was scared to death, and I just wanted to run up to her and protect her from anything negative that the board could have said about her.

I was thankful when the board voted her into another position that would undoubtedly advance her career. I could tell by the relaxing of her shoulders that the vote was a relief to her as well. When the meeting ended, Eric and I stood by the doorway as Tisha spoke to a few others in the room. As she and Amber finally prepared to leave the building, I saw her eyes widen when she spotted me. I looked deeply into her eyes, trying to read her emotions, but all I could see was shock. It was a little discouraging, because I really hoped I'd see appreciation.

"Hi, Tisha," I said, trying to swallow my disappointment.

"Nelson. Hi. What are you doing here?" she asked.

"We'll wait outside for you all," Eric said before grabbing Amber's hand and leading her out of the door.

"Eric and Amber told me about your meeting with the board. I just wanted to come and show my support. Congratulations on the new job," I said, then handed her the flowers. "These are for you."

She sniffed the roses then said, "I don't know what to say. Uh, thanks for the flowers, they're beautiful. And, uh, thanks for coming and being supportive. That was really sweet of you."

"I wasn't trying to be sweet; I was trying to prove to you that I'm serious about you, about us."

Tisha sighed. I sensed her rebuttal before she spoke it. "We've been over this before. You're not the committed type and I'm not sure I am either. And now, I've got this new job and all of this new responsibility. I'm just not sure it could really work between us," she said, her eyes darting everywhere around the room except at me.

I lifted her chin with my index finger to force her to look into my eyes. "When are you going to stop hiding behind your job?"

She pushed my hand away. "What? I'm not hiding behind my job, I'm just saying that—"

I cut her off. "You're just hiding behind your job. You won't let anyone get close to you, and you're using this job as the excuse when really you're just scared."

Tisha laughed. "Oh, so now you're a psychologist?"

"No, I'm a man who really cares about you, and who is trying to build something special with you, but you keep boxing me out."

"Because I'm too busy."

I folded my arms in front of me. I figured she would be difficult, but experiencing her pigheadedness was starting to frustrate me. "Okay, so when was the last time you were not too busy to be in a relationship?"

"I—well, there was . . . It's taken me fifteen years to build my career. I'm always busy," she said defiantly.

I shook my head at her childish thinking. I finally understood how others used to feel when they would try to talk some sense into me about my player ways. Talk about getting a taste of your own medicine.

"And you know what?" I asked. "One of these days, your career is going to be over, and you're going to look around and have absolutely nothing because you invested into nothing except your career. Look at your best friend Amber. She has a very successful career, but she has still managed to make the time for a husband and children. She understands that moving up the corporate ladder isn't everything. Tonight was one of the most critical nights of your career and who were you sitting next to? A married woman who should have been at home with her own family, but instead she had to be here with you because you won't take the time to let a man be there for you. One of these days, Amber's not going to come to your rescue. She's going to be consumed by her own family. Then what are you going to do?"

Tisha appeared flustered by my question. "I don't know, Nelson. I don't know what I'm going to do when Amber isn't there for me. She's always been there, so I've never had to worry about that. Are you happy?"

I reached out and touched her arm. "No, I'm not, but I'm trying to be happy with you if you would just let me."

She pulled away from me. "What do you want from me?"

"I want your heart."

She looked away. "I don't know if that's possible."

I let out an exasperated sigh. "Tisha, I really like you, and I think we could be great together. I know that I'm known for being a jerk, but I'm ready to put all of that craziness and even my player ways aside for the chance to be with you. But I'm not going to chase you forever. You need to make a decision."

I pulled out one of my business cards and began writing on the back of it. "I'm writing down my home address. If you want a real relationship with me, you can find me here." I grabbed her hand and placed the card in the center of her palm. "But I won't be waiting long for you, so you better make up your mind quickly. I hope to see you soon, but if not, I'll understand that you were too busy for me. Congrats again on the promotion."

I walked out of the building, past Amber and Eric, and waited at Eric's car for him to take me home. After a few seconds, Eric got the hint and let me in the car.

"I guess it didn't go too well," Eric said during our drive to my place.

I shrugged. "It went the way it was going to go. Tisha is very headstrong; it's one of the things I admire about her. But she's going to have to make a conscious decision to make time for a man. Any other way isn't going to work, at least not for me."

Eric offered me a brotherly rub on the top of my head. "Nelson, I know we haven't always seen eye to eye, but I have to admit that lately, you've matured a great deal. I'm proud of you for even putting yourself out there for Tisha. You're a good guy, and if she has any sense at all, she'll come around."

"Thanks, bro. I hope you're right. I guess we'll have to wait and see."

A little over two weeks passed with no call, text, or visit from Tisha. At first, I felt strong—she would make the right choice and come to me. But after fifteen days of silence, my confidence plummeted. I sat in the living room on the sofa watching TV feeling sorry for myself. After all of these years of holding a grudge over Charmaine, had I finally opened my heart to another woman just to get rejected? Maybe it was karma for all of the hearts I'd broken along the way. If so, I deserved it so I really couldn't be too mad about it.

"I'm hungry like a slave. You wanna order a pizza?" Sean asked me after rummaging through the kitchen cabinets.

"I could eat. Alright, order one. Get the meat lovers pizza," I said.

Sean called our favorite pizza restaurant and placed an order for two large pizzas to be delivered. Putting his half of the money on the coffee table in front of me, he said, "I need to spend some quality time in the bathroom. Pay for the pizza when it comes."

"Too much information, man!" I yelled at him as he urgently headed down the hallway.

Thirty minutes later, the doorbell rang. I grabbed his money off the table then headed to the front door. I opened the door while pulling my wallet out my back pocket. I expected to see the acne-faced 20-something year old boy who usually delivered our orders, but instead I was greeted by a nervous looking Tisha.

"Tisha? Hey," I said as I let the shock of her presence sink in.

"Hey, Nelson. Is this a bad time?" she asked, peering down and noticing the wad of money in my hand.

"Uh, no. I thought you were the pizza guy. We ordered some pizza, so . . ."

"Oh, okay. Uh, can I come in?"

"Yeah, I'm sorry. Please, come in," I said as I backed away from the door and let her come inside.

I showed her into the living room and we both took a seat on the sofa.

"Nice place," she said.

"Thanks. So, how have you been?" I asked, trying to ease the tension.

"I've been okay. Busy, but you know me." She giggled. "How about you? You been okay?"

"Yeah, I'm hanging in there. Just working and the usual."

"Good, good." She bit her lip then said, "Listen, I came over here today because I've been thinking a lot about what you said after the board meeting. I know that I'm practically married to my career, and up until now, I thought that was what I wanted. But then there was Vegas, and you, and this whole mess with my job. One of the most important lessons that I learned from my career crisis is that jobs and careers are not guaranteed. For so long I put so much into my position because I thought that I would always be able to fall back on it, that if I worked hard it would be the one thing in my life that I could count on. Well, now I see that no matter how hard I work, at any moment, I still could lose it all. I guess what I'm trying to say is that as much as I love what I do, I don't want it to define me. If I am what I do, what happens when I no longer can do it? I'll be completely lost. Getting the rug pulled from under me over the last several months was such an awful feeling. I need to make my life about more than working so that I'll always have something to look forward to. I need to have a better relationship with God, my family, and friends, and I need to have a man in my life who cares enough about me to tell me the truth when I'm too bullheaded to see it for myself."

I grinned. "Are you asking me to be that man?"

She blushed. "Yes, if you'll still have me, I want you to be that man."

"I—"

The doorbell rang, interrupting my response.

I put up my index finger and stood. "One second. Let me get the door. It's probably the pizza guy this time."

I ran to the door, paid for the pizzas, and brought them into the kitchen, laying them down on the countertop. Reentering the living room, I attempted to begin my response again.

"Sorry. I was saying that I—"

Sean burst into the living room. "Is the pizza here? I'm starvin' like Marvin." When he noticed Tisha, he stopped and said, "Oh, hey there."

"Hey," she said.

I rushed through the introductions. "Sean, this is Tisha. Tisha, Sean."

Sean began to laugh. "This is the Tisha? The one who—"

"Sean, really dude? Don't you see us talking?" I couldn't believe this guy.

Sean laughed again. "Oh, my bad. I'll just take my box of pizza and go back to my room."

"Thanks. I appreciate it," I said as I watched him go into the kitchen, grab a box of pizza, and head back toward the bedrooms.

"See ya later, Tisha," he yelled out as he walked out.

"Alright, Sean," she said, humoring him.

"Sorry again," I said, hoping we wouldn't have any more distractions. "Now where were we?"

She smiled, coyly. "You were about to say something."

I inched closer to her. "Right. I was going to say that I would love to be that man for you. But are you sure that you aren't too busy?"

She touch the side of my face. "I promise to never again be too busy to make time for you."

I leaned forward and kissed her gently on the lips. "I can live with that."

Lesson 24: Be Careful What You Ask For

Death and life are in the power of the tongue: and they that
love it shall eat the fruit thereof. (Proverbs 18:21)

Lena

I thought I wanted Douglass to be with someone else until
he actually was. I walked into Starbucks near the hospital
that I worked at, desperately needing a caffeine fix to get me
through the rest of my double shift. I had just finished
ordering an espresso macchiato when I spotted Douglass
seated at a table with a woman who was smiling so hard at
him that I was surprised her face didn't shatter into pieces
when she blinked. Without thinking, I strolled over to their
table. I knew I had no right to act possessive, but there was
no way I was going to be in the same space as him and not
make my presence known.

"Douglass," I said with a fake grin. "What a surprise to see
you here."

"Lena," he said, startled. He had been so engrossed in the
woman that he hadn't noticed me. That made me feel even
worse.

The woman looked back and forth between him and me,
most likely trying to ascertain our relationship. Douglass
observed her confused expression and introduced us.

"Natalie, this is Lena. She works at the hospital across the
street as a nurse. Lena, this is Natalie. She's a masseuse."

Douglass tried to save himself by introducing us by our job titles and not our relationship to him. I had to give him credit for thinking so quickly on his feet.

"A masseuse? Really?" I asked, pretending to be impressed. "Maybe I could get your card. I went to Las Vegas last month and had this awesome massage. It made me think that I should probably pamper myself more often."

"Sure," Natalie said, reaching into her purse and pulling out a business card.

I took the card and tucked it into my purse. "Thanks."

"Lena!" one of the Starbucks workers yelled out—in the nick of time—informing me that my espresso was ready.

I smiled, courteously. "Well, that's me. Douglass, it's good to see you again. And Natalie, I'll be in touch."

It took everything in me not to look back as I picked up my coffee and exited the building.

I couldn't believe that I actually missed Douglass. Two days had passed since our run-in at Starbucks and I couldn't get him out of my head. I started to reminisce about the time we spent together and all of the sweet things he had done for me. The more I thought about it, the more I realized how big of a mistake I made pushing him away from me while I was in Vegas. I understood that my focus on Eric made it impossible for me to be satisfied with any other man. In my mind, I had Eric on a pedestal, but it was time for him to come down. I wanted my own life with my own husband, not to be fixated on someone else's.

I was on my way over to Eric's house to pick up Jonelle from her weekend visitation when I decided to stop playing games and give Douglass a call. He was a decent guy, and if I ever wanted to get married again, I would have to stop sabotaging my relationships with men and be willing to make myself vulnerable to someone other than the father of my child.

Douglass answered on the third ring. "Lena?"

I smiled at the sound of his voice. "Hi, Doug. How are you?"

"I'm cool. I didn't expect to hear from you. Did you need something?"

"Uh, actually, I do," I said. "I wanted to apologize for what I said to you when I was in Vegas. I had a lot going on at the time and I was mean to you. You've been really kind and good to me, and I should have treated you so much better. I'm really sorry."

"Oh, wow. Okay," he said, sounding surprised. "Apology accepted. Thanks for admitting that."

The moment he forgave me I felt a zillion times better. I was a bit nervous that he would respond negatively, but was glad that he wasn't harboring any ill feelings. "It felt really good to say that. Sort of a relief," I confessed.

"Apologizing can be that way. Lena, I am about to head out to a meeting. I don't want to seem rude by rushing you off the phone, but was there anything else?"

I had my man back. What else could I want at that moment? "No, we're good. You can come by later on if you want. I think I'm going to fry fish tonight. I know you like tilapia."

He hesitated, then said, "Uh, I don't think that's a good idea."

"Why not?"

"Because I'm dating someone else now, Natalie. The woman you met at the coffee shop the other day."

I gasped. As much as I thought there might be some resentment between us, I never imagined he would try to replace me . . . so quickly. "You're serious about her?"

"Yeah. We've only been hanging out for a few weeks, but I really like her and she wants a committed relationship with me. You said you wanted me to find someone else. I thought you meant it, so I did."

Of course. It's all my fault. Throw it in my face, why don't you. "But it has only been a month. Who gets out of a relationship and finds another that quickly?"

"Technically, we weren't in a relationship, as you often reminded me. Lena, you're a great woman and I enjoyed spending time with you, but I've moved on. Honestly, I don't know if you really want me or saw me with Natalie and this is a jealousy thing. Either way, I'm happy now and I'm not going to give up the good thing I have to go back to playing games with you."

"But I'm not playing games anymore," I said, almost in tears.

"Good for you. Lena, I'm going to be late if I don't leave now, so good luck and I'll see you around."

"But—"

I wasn't ready for the conversation to end, but my phone made a noise as if the call had ended. "Hello?" I said, then looked at the phone when I didn't get an immediate response.

He had hung up on me.

How in the world did I go from being the woman of his dreams to being the woman getting brushed off? Before I could calm myself down, my emotions got the best of me and I began to cry. Was my life really this pitiful? How could I keep making so many mistakes?

I sobbed the rest of the way to Eric's house. He was outside checking the mailbox and noticed me pulling up. He waved and jogged up to the car. I didn't want him to see my puffy eyes, but there wasn't enough time to get myself together before he reached me. I wiped away the tears on my cheek as he approached the car. He was smiling, but when he saw my wreck of a face, his smile disappeared.

My car windows were rolled up because I had the air conditioning on blast. They called our area Hotlanta for a reason. Eric knocked on my window when I didn't automatically roll it down. I huffed and reluctantly rolled down the window.

"Are you alright?" he asked, sounding sincere.

I sniffled. "I will be."

He place his elbow on the roof on my car and leaned against the car. "What happened?"

I really didn't want to discuss my love life with Eric so I kept my reply short. "Me. I happened."

"What does that mean?"

"It means that I am my own worst enemy. I keep messing up and having to pay the price for my mistakes."

He glanced up at his house then said, "I know we're not all that close anymore, but do you want to come inside and talk?"

I sniffled again. "No. I'm sure Amber's seen enough of me this summer. Just go get Jonelle and I'll leave."

"Lena, even though we've had our differences over the years, I still care about you and what happens to you. You're the mother of one of my children, and at one time, we were friends. I don't want you to leave here without letting me know what's going on with you. Maybe I can help."

Why couldn't he leave well enough alone? I needed a friend at that moment, someone who cared, but Eric was not my first pick or my last. "You can't help me with this problem, especially since you're a part of it."

"Then that's all the more reason to talk to me. What did I do? What's the matter?"

As much as I never planned to pour my heart out to Eric, who else was begging to console me? I could tell that he wasn't going to let up, so I let him in. "Eric, I went to Las Vegas this summer with you all because I thought I could win you back. I thought that maybe if I was around you again in a different environment, that you would see what a mistake you made by marrying Amber instead of me. I was fooling myself. You love Amber, not me. And truthfully, I don't love you either, not really. I think I was just in love with the idea of having our family back together—you, me, and Jonelle. I always thought it would be us, despite how I acted or what I said. When you married Amber, you took the possibility of us away from me. I was just trying to get it back.

"I've been dating men for years, trying to make them you, but they aren't. And when I realize they can't be you, I push them away. Unfortunately, I recently pushed away a man that I really care about, someone who was really good to me. Now, it's too late. He has found someone else and again, I lose. I'm the one left standing outside in the cold alone while everyone else gets their happily ever after. Eric, what's wrong with me? Why can't I be happy too?" Before I knew it, I was crying again.

Eric stood up straight, pushing himself off the car. *He's probably ready to run away now*, I thought. I waited for Eric to make an excuse to go back inside the house and get Jonelle, but he remained standing there, gaping at me.

"Uh, this is kind of awkward," I said to him after a good thirty seconds or so had passed without a word.

"Lena," Eric said. "Get out of the car."

"What? Why?"

"Just get out of the car for a second."

I was confused, but I unlocked my door and got out of the vehicle. I stood in front of him completely dumbfounded about his request.

He took my hand and squeezed it gently. "Lena, there's nothing wrong with you. You could use an attitude adjustment at times, but that doesn't mean you're unworthy of love. I dated you back in the day because you were a wonderful woman, and you still are. I'm not the man for you, but I'm 100 percent sure that God has the perfect guy for you, and in His time, you'll experience the companionship you desire. Until then, know that you are a part of this family and we love you— Amber too."

I frowned. "Amber doesn't love me."

"Amber loves you, she just doesn't like you most of the time. Two different things."

I laughed. "Yeah, I haven't made it easy for her to like me. I'm going to work on being kinder . . . and less sneaky. Thanks for what you just said, Eric. I really needed to hear it."

"I'm not just saying it. I mean it. Now, come over here and give me a hug, then we're going inside and you're going to hug Amber too," he said, firmly.

"Hold up now—"

"You just said you were going to be kinder. This is how kindness starts. Hug me."

Eric opened his arms and I entered his embrace. It was therapeutic to be hugged by him. I was a little nervous that in the middle of our hug Amber would come outside and a whole dramatic scene would commence, but that never occurred. Instead, he walked me inside of the house, took me into Amber's office, and said, "Amber, Lena wants you to hug her. She's ready to be a part of this family."

Amber looked up at me from her seated position behind her desk. I didn't know if she would laugh or yell at Eric's statement, but she did neither. She stood up, traveled over to me, and pulled me into her arms. She smelled like a mixture of fruity body spray and baby powder. For some reason, I found myself relaxing in her embrace and crying again.

Really, Lena?

I would have to get my emotions in check. But for those few minutes, I let myself just feel.

August

Epilogue
Lesson 25: What God Has for You is for You

So shall my word be that goeth forth out of my mouth: it shall not return unto me void, but it shall accomplish that which I please, and it shall prosper in the thing whereto I sent it. (Isaiah 55:11)

Nelson

Life was good. I had a good woman in my life who challenged me to be better. With all of the talk about Tisha's promotion, I started to consider my own career. I had been working in the information technology field for almost twenty years. My current job was a video game programmer. I mainly worked with quality assurance, testing new games for glitches and other weaknesses. I also helped create game updates when newer versions of games were needed. Before meeting Tisha, I was cool with my job. I made good money and my job was easy. Yet after a few discussions about my career with Tisha, I realized that somewhere along the line I had settled. There was nothing wrong with my job, but I had stopped looking for opportunities to advance and simply become comfortable with just being employed.

"If you could do anything and if money wasn't an option, what would you do?" Tisha asked me.

I shrugged. "I don't know. I've never thought about it."

"I realize that could be a hard question, so let me rephrase it," she said. "If you could do anything else outside of what you're doing now, what would you do?"

I thought about her question for several seconds then said, "I guess I would create a couple new video games. I've had a few ideas over the years, but I just haven't taken the time to develop them and figure out how to sell them. With my job now, I work with games that have already been created, so all I'm doing is perfecting someone else's idea. But I think it would be cool to be the actual designer of games, or at least one game."

Her eyes lit up. "Do they have jobs like that at your company?"

"Honestly, most major IT advancement happens in Silicon Valley. I'm just not interested in moving to California. There are plenty of companies like the one I work for all over the country, but the Santa Clara Valley is where most people go who really want to make big moves. My employer doesn't create games in-house. Larger companies hire us to develop their games. To answer your question, I could design the concept for a new game and then sell it to a major company, or I could make the entire game myself and do everything independently," I said.

"I can tell you've thought about this before."

I nodded. "I have, but I'm not sure that I'm ready to do all of the work required to create the game and turn around and try to package and distribute it. If I had the chance to do either, I'd rather just design the concept and even write the codes, but let a company with the resources do the rest."

"Can you design a game and continue to work for your current employer?"

"Yeah. The only way it would impact my job is if I started making a lot of money designing games and no longer had the time to do both."

Tisha smiled at me. "So why don't you give it a shot? Keep working at your job, but in your free time, start developing some of your ideas."

She made it all sound so easy. I had considered the idea plenty of times, but it always felt as if it would be too much of a challenge. Having someone in my life who pushed me to aim higher made what used to be intimidating seem somewhat manageable. "I might just do that. I guess since I have a girlfriend who's a powerhouse, I'll have to step up my ambitions."

She leaned in and kissed me on my forehead. "No, not really. You just be you. If you would have said your current job was everything you wanted, I would be okay with that. However, if there is anything else you want to make happen in this life, I'm willing to support you in that as well."

We'd all grown in such a short yet intense period of time. I was no long scared of monogamy, Tisha stopped running from herself (and me), Owen had finally set a wedding date for next year, and Sky . . . well, Sky was still hitting on younger men. Three out of four was pretty good in my book.

That night, I officially threw away my player card. I literally had a laminated card in my wallet with my name on it that said THE PLAYER'S CLUB. The moment Tisha left my place, I took the card out of my wallet and tossed it in the garbage. I then found a three-ring notebook and started jotting down some of the game ideas that had been swirling around in my head over the past few years. The more I thought about it, the more I was sure that my best days were yet to come.

Tisha

In August, I officially took on my new job at the Board of Education. I wasn't sure how the transition would go both for me and for my former school, but I stepped out in faith, believing that it would all work out in the end. I'm happy to say that it did.

One of my former assistant principals at Turner Hill High was put in the position of interim principal while the BOE went through the job selection process. Whatever decision was made, it would not be implemented until the following school year. From time to time, I stopped in to see how things were going and offer any support I could to the interim principal. I missed my staff and students greatly, but as with any change, I let go of what was behind me for the hope of what was in front of me.

My new role as executive director of leadership was extremely challenging. Although many of my job skills were transferable, I was working in a completely new role and had to do a 180 degree adjustment of mindset to tackle the duties of my new position. Over time, the job became easier and my confidence increased as I started to acclimate. My supervisor, staff, and even the superintendent, Dr. Cooper, were all helpful in my successful transition. Every day wasn't perfect, but it was amazing to have the opportunity to impact the school system on a broader level. Each week, I witnessed staff and students lives being positively influenced by my actions. I felt truly blessed, and I had no doubt about where my blessing flowed from.

In addition to my new job, I had a new romantic relationship with Nelson. Who would have ever guessed Nelson and I would end up as a couple? I thought back to that plane trip to Las Vegas and how angry I was that I had to sit next to him. Back then, I didn't know the real Nelson. Yeah, he can still be a jerk from time to time, but for the most part, he has a good heart and he's a great friend. We're taking the relationship slow and getting to know each other for now. But you never know . . . maybe wedding bells are in our future. Neither he nor I are worried about marriage at the moment. We're too busy building our careers, developing our friendship, and falling in love with living the single life!

Lena

Jonelle's birthday bash turned out to be a huge success. I wish I could say that it was all due to me, but that would be a lie. During the Las Vegas trip, I had practically depleted my savings, which meant that I no longer had money set aside for her party. The invitations had gone out in May, and Jonelle was super excited about having a party at Six Flags, so it was too late to cancel. I attempted to work as much as possible to make up for the lost funds, but with it being summer, school being out, and Jonelle staying with me during the weekdays, my available work time was limited. I wanted to take advantage of my time with her. I didn't want her entire summer to pass without us enjoying it because I always had to work. This was the life of a single parent, and it was in these moments that I understood why partnering with Eric was so vital.

Following our heartfelt experience that day in July, I ended up coming clean with Eric and Amber about the overwhelming expenses of the birthday party. We ended up agreeing that they would pay for the majority of the party, but we all would take equal credit for hosting it. The way Amber explained, as her mother, father, and stepmother, each person would contribute 33.3 percent toward the cost of the event, therefore we all would be equally responsible. Now that Amber and I were sort of allies, I appreciated her savvy business skills. I guess Amber wasn't that bad after all.

"Happy birthday to you! Happy birthday to you! Happy birthday, dear Jonelle. Happy birthday to you!" everyone sang as Jonelle smiled at her two-tier, pink and white, *Hello Kitty* cake. The group of thirty-five adults and children broke out into applause and cheers when she blew out all fourteen candles. I almost cried at the sight of my little-big girl growing up, but I forced myself to calm down.

I kissed her on the cheek and asked the question you're not supposed to ask. "What did you wish for, sweetie?"

Jonelle looked up at me apprehensively, then said, "I wished for a sister. E. J. is cute, but I want a baby sister. My friend Jasmine has a baby sister and she's soooo much fun to play with. Mommy, are you going to have another girl?"

I felt my face flush with embarrassment. Everyone at the party was looking at me as if I held my daughter's dreams in my womb. I was getting older and I hadn't planned on having any more children. Even if I wanted more kids, I wasn't married or even dating anyone seriously. I couldn't believe she had put me on the spot like that.

"Sweetheart, Mommy isn't—" I started, but was cut off by Eric.

"Jonelle, Amber and I have a surprise for you."

"You do?" Jonelle and I asked in unison.

He turned and glanced at Amber who nodded at him and smiled. Eric looked back at Jonelle and said, "We were going to wait until things were further along to break the news, but in light of Jonelle's wish, we may as well spill the beans. Amber's pregnant and you're going to have another sibling in about seven months. Hopefully, you'll get your wish and it will be a girl."

"Yay!" Jonelle squealed.

"What?" I cried.

As the other adults at the party began to crowd around Amber and Eric, offering congratulations, I felt the life drain out of me. Mr. and Mrs. Perfect were having another child. They were going to give Jonelle the family she wanted, not me. I watched her run over to her daddy and stepmom and hug them tightly. I know I had agreed to be kinder and a team player with the Hayeses, but once again, they seemed to win, and somehow, I was shut out with the losers. Everyone who had attended that singles conference was in a better place, including Nelson and Tisha. Even Jessica had worked out her relationship with her man and now they were getting married. Why was I the only one still waiting for my time to shine? Promise or no promise, I wouldn't stand around and watch Eric and Amber have all of the happiness in the world while I couldn't catch a break to save my life.

Another baby?

I grabbed the large kitchen knife I had brought with me and began to cut the cake forcefully. I knew I should have hosted the party by myself and not took a dime from Eric or his wife. After aggressively cutting up the cake, I forced myself to calm down. I was still upset by Eric and Amber's announcement, but I'd worked too hard at pulling the party together for my daughter and I wasn't going to let anyone ruin the accomplishment for me. In a perfect world, we would all be one big happy family, just like Eric wanted. But our world was far from perfect. I had to accept that I might not ever be happy for the Hayeses, especially when their victories always shined light on my defeats. It was at that moment that I realized that although I had not taken that stupid rock home from the singles conference, I had brought something else home that might take a long time to fix—a very broken Lena.

I looked up from the cake and saw Eric walking towards me. Attempting to demonstrate self-control, I took a deep breath and said, "Congratulations."

Eric smiled and said, "Thanks, but there is actually something else I wanted to talk to you about."

My heart plummeted. What else could the man want from me? To be their surrogate?

"The Woods called us last night. They're putting together an event next year and wanted to know if we'd be interested in participating. All of us, including you and Jonelle," he said.

"Me? What kind of event requires all of us to be there?" I asked, feeling confused.

"It's a family event that focuses on parenting. Another set of Bible study classes related to relationship building. They're calling it Parents 101."

"What about the baby? Didn't you all just announce that Amber's pregnant?"

"They're scheduling it for next September. Amber will have already had the baby by then. Plus, it's going to be in New York City and that's where Amber is from. It'll give us an excuse to take the kids to visit her family up there. We'd love to have you join us, and we're willing to cover all of the expenses for you . . . and Jonelle, of course. We think it would be a good experience for Jonelle to see us all working together, away from home, doing something fun—sort of like a family vacation. Will you come?"

As much as I didn't want to spend any more time with the Hayeses, a free trip to NYC was a very tempting offer. I'd never been there before and it was on my bucket list of things to do.

"Okay," I said. "I'll go for Jonelle's sake."

Eric smiled and nodded. "Thanks . . . for Jonelle's sake."

As he walked away, I thought about the invitation. New York. The Big Apple. The *real* city that never sleeps. If this upcoming trip was anything at all like Las Vegas, I wondered if our dysfunctional, blended family could tolerate being together in New York . . . and even more so, if New York could tolerate us. We'd just have to wait and see.

Author's Note & Acknowledgements

I enjoyed taking the characters in *Couples 101* to South Beach so much that when I considered the next book in the series, *Singles 101*, I was sure that I also wanted the location to be somewhere exciting. The moment I closed my eyes and asked, "Where should I take this singles conference?" the answer came to me so quickly that I had a difficult time accepting it as the right choice. Las Vegas, Nevada. I thought I was taking it too far, and went to God several times for another location. But each and every time, Las Vegas was whispered to me, so finally, I embraced Sin City as the location for *Singles 101*.

Four books into the Wife 101 Series and I am still amazed that the storyline continues to grow and develop with the lives of the characters. After writing *Wife 101*, several of my readers voiced a desire to see Tisha get a man or take one of the Woods' relationship-based courses. She was such a fun character to write that I also wanted to see more of her at some point in the series. When the idea to write *Singles 101* emerged during the process of penning *Husband 101*, I instantly knew that Tisha would be best for the protagonist role. After *Husband 101*, Nelson was also a memorable character for me, and I pictured a love-hate relationship between his character and Tisha. But I was not prepared for Lena returning to play a significant role in *Singles 101*. As I sat down to start writing, I intended to create a new character as the third point of view, but Lena literally (pun intended) came out of nowhere and demanded the third spot. She was the hardest character to write in this book because her actions were constantly different than I imagined. In this series, I've always attempted to complete each character's arc, but Lena would not allow me to just give her a truly satisfying ending. Against all of my personal writing and reading preferences, the book ends with Lena unable to let bygones be bygones. Needless to say, Lena will return with Amber and Eric in the fifth book of the series, *Parents 101*.

Of all of the books in the series, *Singles 101* feels the edgiest. Most Christian fiction books avoid the description of worldly ideas and concepts for the sake of providing a clean, inspiring, and Christ-focused work. In my writing, I try to stay within the confines of what is expected in Christian fiction, toeing the line at times, but mostly staying away from the boarder. *Singles 101* toes the line much more than I intended with the characters enjoying clubbing, parties, secular music, gambling, and whatnot. Because the book takes place in Las Vegas, and due to the characters themselves being on the troubled characters list in the series (Believers who live worldly lives), it would have been unrealistic and unauthentic to have Tisha, Nelson, and Lena visit Vegas and act like angels. I pray that their experiences in Las Vegas do not glorify worldly behavior, but provide a small peek into the energy and nature of a city infamous for its sinful environment.

I would like to thank the readers who faithfully follow the Wife 101 Series. Your feedback, reviews, emails, Facebook messages, tweets, and words of encouragement keep me committed to this series when at times I want to start something completely new and abandon writing about relationship and personal development classes within the world of fiction.

Thanks to my mother, Kathleen Wilson, and my family and friends whose support is invaluable to me: Darius Harmon, Tanisha Smith, TaNisha Webb, Sherryle Kiser Jackson, Sharon Bruner, Kesha Lee, Shauna Taylor, Sharitta Gross, Clarissa Johnson, Coretta Cotton, and everyone whose name I haven't forgotten, but don't have the space to include.

Thank you to my Divine Garden Press family who continues to grow as God brings wonderful people with amazing stories into our lives.

Thank you to my editor, Michelle Chester. You've been such a blessing. Your feedback and attention to the details helps my writing shine. You rock!

Thanks to Regina Harris for the insight on school systems.

Thanks to the reviewers and book clubs that have taken the time to read this series and to share it with others. Special thanks to OOSA Book Club, KC Girlfriends Book Club, Tiffany Craig from Reading in Black and White, Candler County Book Club, Black Pearls Greenwood, Readers Block Book Club, and the many other book clubs that I've had the privilege of meeting and sharing my work with.

Most importantly, all praises to God for continuing to use me as a vessel for Your glory. Thank You for calling me, loving me, and choosing me even though I make mistakes (over and over again). You see me in my perfected state and never give up on me. Help me to reflect Your light into this dark world so that others would be drawn to You.

If you enjoyed this book, please remember to review it and to tell others about it.

Happy Reading,

Andrea

Singles 101: The Playlist

With the exception of my novel *Spell* (Janell), I usually don't insert too much music or even listen to music while writing. But in *Singles 101*, taking the characters to Las Vegas and having them hang out at several clubs/parties, I couldn't ignore their need for decent party music. I have to admit that I've been out of the club scene for years now and rarely listen to the radio. I'm starting to feel like older people who mispronounce musicians' names and complain about "all that racket." After writing *Couples 101*, I went on a cruise and ended up hearing a lot of new music on the ship. I felt so out-of-date with the current music and had no idea who many of the artists were, but after a week of hearing the same songs, a few of the beats stuck with me. As I wrote *Singles 101* and visualized the characters at the various secular venues, some of the music from my cruise returned to my memory. Feeling inspired, I began to research other songs that are likely to be heard inside Las Vegas nightclubs. Most of the music played in Las Vegas is House and Techno, but a lot of party music also has Hip Hop, Pop, and R&B influences. I ended up creating a playlist during the last couple days of writing the novel so that I could motivate myself to finish the project, and give you, the reader, additional insight into the music floating through my head during the creation of this book. My listing of this music is not in promotion of these artists or songs, but for the sake of bringing you the full experience of Las Vegas. Enjoy!

1. Where Have You Been by Rhianna
2. Happy by Pharrell Williams
3. Party Rock by LMFAO
4. Right Round by Flo Rida
5. Firework by Katy Perry
6. Wobble by V.I.C.
7. Shots by Lil' Jon Featuring LMFAO
8. Bulletproof by David Guetta Featuring Sia
9. We Found Love by Rhianna
10. 1999 by Prince
11. I Gotta Feeling by Black Eyed Peas
12. Low by Flo Rida
13. Dynamite by Taio Cruz
14. Sexy and I Know It by LMFAO
15. Poker Face by Lady Gaga
16. Scream by Usher

Reading Group Guide

1. Singlehood encompasses a variety of personal circumstances (i.e., single with children, divorced, widowed, engaged, dating, etc.). Which character in *Singles 101* is most like you? Which character is least like you? Why?

2. The singles conference takes place in Las Vegas, Nevada. Do you think this was a good idea or bad idea considering the goals of the event organizers?

3. The main characters of the book indulge in gambling, clubbing, and drinking while in Las Vegas. How do you feel about their behaviors while attending a faith-based conference? Do you think their actions positively or negatively influenced their experience and/or development during the conference?

4. Tisha has a work related issue in which she chooses to fight rather than walk away from her employer. Do you think she made the right choice? Should she have accepted the final offer? Why or why not?

5. Nelson loses someone he cares about which causes him to realize his unresolved pain. Discuss his emotional and behavioral changes after the loss, and how much it influenced his ability to trust women again.

6. Lena attends the conference in hopes of having fun and getting close to her ex-boyfriend. What could Lena have done differently during her trip and afterwards that would have given her a more positive life outcome?

7. Romantic sparks fly between Nelson and Tisha. Do you think they will work well as a couple? Why or why not?

8. Each day, the conference participants are required to attend a Singles 101 class instructed by Martin and Lydia Woods. Of the five Singles 101 classes in the book, which class impacted you most? Why?

9. Each day, the conference participants are offered a wide range of workshops they can attend. Fragments of four of these sessions are including in the novel. Of the four workshops presented in the book, which workshop did you value most? Why?

10. Were you satisfied with the ending for each of the three main characters—Tisha, Nelson, and Lena? Why or why not?

Wife 101
The Wife 101 Series, Book 1

Final Exam Question #1
Is an independent woman destined to remain single forever or can a wife training course turn a mess into a Mrs.?

Thriving Atlanta mogul Amber Ross thinks she is the perfect woman. But when she finds out that her recent ex-boyfriend is marrying someone else, she begins to question what men really want. Frustrated with the dating scene and her failing interactions with men, Amber enrolls in a course at her church geared towards teaching women how to be effective in their relationships: Wife 101. Amber expects the class to shed some light on her courting flaws, but it does more than that; it challenges many of her life choices and ideas about romance. Her new attitude brings unexpected love, but has she learned enough to make the right choices and snag a great husband, or like a foolish woman, will she tear down her home with her own hands?

Husband 101

The Wife 101 Series, Book 2

Final Exam Question #2
How many women does it take to ruin a marriage?

Eric Hayes is a man with too many women in his life. As a bachelor, he loved all of the attention, but now being a married man, he quickly realizes that he cannot please more than one woman at a time. Succumbing to the pressure, Eric takes a course at his wife's church to become better equipped for the bittersweet realities of marriage: Husband 101. The course ends up being more than he bargained for and his role and actions as a man are put to the test, one that he struggles to pass. Unable to keep everyone satisfied, Eric's picture-perfect life begins to crumble even before he can make it to his first anniversary. Will he heed to good advice and put into practice the lessons that can salvage his family, or will pride and self-reliance guarantee his fall?

Couples 101

The Wife 101 Series, Book 3

Final Exam Question #3
Can six couples with a boatload of issues survive on the hottest beach in the USA?

Amber and Eric are back in the third installment of the Wife 101 Series, and they are bringing some old friends, plus a few new ones, along for the ride! When relationship educators Martin and Lydia Woods decided to host their church's first marriage retreat on Miami's sultry South Beach, they expected it to be eventful, yet they got much more than anticipated. With the help of psychologist Dr. Andrea Wilson, the couple is prepared to teach the art of war by placing their pupils in an environment full of people, parties, and forbidden pleasures.

Amber and Eric are nearing their second anniversary. Their relationship would be smooth sailing, but Amber's empty womb is causing tension both in and out of the bedroom. Eric's friend Carl and his wife, Kelly, just wanted a vacation. But when the lights and music of South Beach beckon for Kelly, will her desire to reclaim her youth lead to the detriment of her marriage? Amber's pastor and first lady, Franklin and Tamela Day, are also on deck, as well as Sarah from the Wife 101 course and her hubby, Jordan. With five couples to counsel, Dr. Wilson certainly has her hands full. Nevertheless, when unforeseen financial issues surface in her own marriage, will she still be able to help her new clients, or will her own husband be the iceberg that sinks her career?

Prayer at sunrise, playtime at sunset, and even a picture perfect dinner cruise, this retreat is guaranteed to be a week these couples will never forget—for better or for worse.

VISIT **WWW.DIVINEGARDENPRESS.COM** AND
LIKE US ON FACEBOOK AT
WWW.FACEBOOK.COM/DIVINEGARDENPRESS
TO FIND OUT MORE ABOUT OUR CURRENT
AND UPCOMING TITLES, AUTHORS, AND
SPECIAL PROMOTIONS!

About the Author

Photograph by Antonio Cleveland

A'ndrea J. Wilson, Ph.D. is the award-winning author of both fiction and nonfiction books, including the novels, *Wife 101, Husband 101, and Couples 101.* She holds a Bachelor's of Science in Psychology, a Master's of Science in Counseling Psychology; Marriage and Family Therapy, and a Doctorate in Global Leadership; Educational Leadership. A'ndrea works as a college professor, as well as conducts workshops on a variety of personal and professional topics. Dr. Wilson is the President of Divine Garden Press, a publishing company that specializes in books addressing marriage and family issues. A native of Rochester, New York, she currently resides in Georgia.

Please visit her online at www.andreawilsononline.com and www.wife101.com or email her at drajwilson@gmail.com.